Split
Bamboo

Leon Phillips

D0877396

SCHOLASTIC BOOK SERVICES
NEW YORK • TORONTO • LONDON • AUCKLAND • SYDNEY • TOKYO

Copyright © 1966 by Doubleday & Company, Inc. This edition is published by Scholastic Book Services, a division of Scholastic Magazines, Inc., by arrangement with Doubleday and Company, Inc.

18 17 16 15 14 13 12 11 10 9 8 7   5 6 7 8 9/7 0/8

Printed in the U.S.A.

For
Margot and Paul

1

THE QUIET of the nuclear submarine was eerie, almost menacing.

Her engines made no sound, although she cut swiftly through the Yellow Sea, more than one hundred and fifty feet below the surface of the water, and there was no sense of motion inside the ship. Somewhere off to the east lay the divided land of Korea, where American-supported troops of the south and the Communists of the north watched each other across the barbed-wire frontier. To the west stood the coast of mainland China, the world's largest Red nation.

But the atmosphere in the tiny cabin of the U.S.S. *Shark* was deceptively serene. Larry Heddon stretched out on the soft foam rubber of his bunk, listening to the faint, hissing noise of the air conditioner overhead as it pumped in man-made fresh air. Trim, and in physical condition that much younger men might have envied, he closed his eyes and ran strong fingers through his brown hair, which was just beginning to turn gray at the temples.

He couldn't sleep, of course, and knew it. After five long years of waiting he was about to embark on the most dangerous adventure of his life. The smallest slip, the most insignificant error in judgment, could prove fatal. He had tried to absorb so much information that he felt drained, his mind blank. Perhaps it had been wrong for a man of forty to accept the assignment.

A deep voice suddenly filtered through the squawk box set in the bulkhead only a few inches from his head. "Will the guest come to the bridge, please? Skipper wants to see you."

Larry rose to his feet, stretched, and tucked the tails of his khaki shirt under the belt of his trousers. The brass in Washington had spent days trying to decide what he should be called on this voyage. Finally General Hopkins had ordered that he was to have no name at all, and the admirals had agreed. So the officers and men of the *Shark* knew him only as "the guest." Even Captain Richards, the sub's commander, had wisely asked no embarrassing questions.

Smiling to himself, Larry made his way along the narrow corridors, twisting and turning through the maze until he reached the bridge. Two young officers and three enlisted men were seated before a huge electronically controlled console, watching tiny lights blinking and occasionally turning knobs and calmly punching buttons. Behind them stood the captain, the silver eagles of his rank gleaming at both sides of his collar.

He motioned toward the rear of the stainless-steel platform, out of the others' earshot. "We're well into the Gulf of Po Hai now," he said, "and we've already passed Yehsien Bay."

Larry glanced at his watch. "When do we arrive off Tientsin?"

"If there's no trouble, around ten P.M., right on schedule. Look at the radar screen. There's a lot of shipping above us, so I don't intend to surface until the last minute."

Everything was going according to plan, and Larry nodded.

"Do you want another meal? The cook is standing by in the galley."

"Thanks all the same, but I had a big steak for dinner. I'd better get ready."

Captain Richards seemed completely relaxed. Nothing in his attitude indicated that he knew the Chinese would drop dozens — even hundreds — of depth bombs in order to blow his ship out of the water if they discovered he was sailing so close to their shore. "I'll give you fifteen minutes' warning before we surface. Enough time?"

"Plenty, thanks." Larry spoke casually too,

7

but his manner changed when he reached his own cabin.

Grim and purposeful now, he unlocked the metal footlocker no one else had been allowed to touch since he had left the secret intelligence training camp in the Pennsylvania hills. He stripped, then began to dress in clothes he took from the locker. His tunic and trousers were made of wool and were well cut, but their color was a dull, almost dirty gray. He checked an automatic revolver of Chinese manufacture and slipped it into a hidden inner pocket made for the purpose. Then he dropped several spare clips of ammunition into another pocket before bending down to tap the heel of a heavy leather boot. The hilt of a double-edged knife, five inches long and razor-sharp, moved into the open, a fraction of an inch from its hiding place, and Larry removed the blade. He turned it over in the palm of his hand several times, then sighed quietly and slid it out of sight again. With luck, he wouldn't have to use any of his weapons.

He took a long time carefully going through a sheaf of papers that he carried in a Russian-made wallet. All of them identified him as Richard L. Bliss, naturalized Chinese citizen, and his photograph appeared on most. One testified that he was a member in good standing of the Communist party. Another was his identity card, and a third permitted him to travel anywhere he pleased in China. These were the most important, and all carried impressive official seals. The people in the credentials-forging department at the Pennsylvania intelligence headquarters had done a perfect job.

Larry carefully stowed away the papers and wallet, then slipped into a shapeless coat of gray padded cotton. Before donning the round visored hat that virtually all officials of the Red Chinese government wore he looked at himself in the mirror set into the bulkhead, feeling a distinct sense of shock when he saw his own reflection. It was still a weird sensation after all these weeks to see a strange face peering back at him instead of his own. And he couldn't help being startled that the face was that of Richard L. Bliss, American turncoat now employed in China's intelligence service.

Touching the tiny scars that were almost invisible at his hairline, Larry realized that the plastic surgeons had performed near miracles. Even his nose had been transformed, and his chin was no longer his own. He was still grateful that his eyes were the same color as Bliss's, so he didn't have to wear tinted contact lenses.

Turning away from the mirror abruptly, he spent the next half hour studying maps of Tientsin and Peking. He had already memorized every last detail, but the maps would have

9

to be left behind and he couldn't afford to take any risks. However, he comforted himself with the thought that neither city had changed much in the years since he had last seen them. China was the only major nation on earth that had engaged in few new building projects since World War II. So, with luck, he'd know his way.

He hadn't been much older then than David was right now when he had first seen China. But he couldn't let himself think of his son, much less hope that he might see the boy in the next few days, and so he busied himself with the maps again.

The squawk box interrupted him. "Fifteen minutes!"

Larry jammed on his hat and took an already packed canvas overnight bag from the footlocker. In it were shaving things and other toilet articles, a clean shirt, and, a final touch for the sake of authenticity, several items of dirty laundry. Everything was of Chinese make and had been smuggled out of the country soon after his mission had been planned. It was good to know that there were friends in China, if he needed them. But he couldn't let himself forget General Hopkins' instructions: "Don't go to the underground for help unless it's urgently necessary. We don't have enough people in China to take the chance of losing them."

The overnight bag in one hand, Larry walked quickly through the sub to the ladder that led to the "sail," the finlike superstructure. Several members of the *Shark*'s crew looked at him curiously, but none seemed surprised. Apparently they had been speculating among themselves that "the guest" would be landed somewhere in Communist territory.

Captain Richards, clad now in a hooded poncho of dull dark gray that would reflect no light, was waiting at the foot of the steel ladder. "It's ten o'clock — on the nose," he said, and led the way to the top.

Two seamen turned electronically powered wheels, and Larry followed Richards onto the tiny open deck of the *Shark,* still dripping with encrusted salt water after the long voyage beneath the surface of the Pacific Ocean.

A strong cold wind blew down from the northwest out of the vast plains of Inner Mongolia, and both men shivered involuntarily, but they were too busy surveying the scene to pay real attention to their discomfort. Off to the right, around a bend, was the main part of the harbor of Tientsin. Long wharves and docks of concrete and steel jutted out into the water, and beyond them stood the older, sagging wharves of wood. Scores of ships rode at anchor, all of them smudged shapes in the distance. Larry supposed that a trained expert like Richards could even now distinguish war-

11

ships from passenger vessels and freighters.

The immediate area was deserted, and the warehouses that lined the shore directly ahead were dark, as were the jagged rocks of the outer harbor limits to the left. Even the weather was cooperating, just as the meteorologists at the Pennsylvania camp had predicted after studying the data relayed by weather observation satellites. The night sky was heavy and overcast, and a light drizzle was falling.

A steady round of explosions sounded from the main harbor waterfront, and both men standing on the deck of the *Shark* knew that they had kept precisely to their schedule. This was the Chinese New Year, and firecrackers were being set off in batches every fifteen seconds. The government frowned on celebrations of the ancient holiday, but the public demand was so strong that officials from Peking permitted a mild demonstration. Larry and Richards had been told that no skyrockets or other night-lighting fireworks would be fired, and there were none. But the captain was on edge, understandably. Every minute he spent here increased the risk to his men and ship.

Several sailors lowered a rubber boat into the water, and Richards held out his hand to Larry. "Good luck."

"Thanks."

"I don't know, and don't want to know, what you intend to do here. But I admire your courage." The captain hesitated for an instant. "When you get back to the States look me up — and we'll get together for dinner."

Larry appreciated the gesture, knowing what the officer was trying to say. "It's a date. My treat." Not waiting for a reply, he climbed down a ladder into the little rubber boat.

Every precaution had been taken, every move rehearsed. A flick of a finger turned on the engine of a small but powerful outboard motor that had been made for just such landings and was unusually quiet. Larry started toward the shore, the noise of the exploding firecrackers muffling the purr of the engine. A coil of nylon rope dyed blue-green to blend with the sea spun out behind him, and he knew that Richards, watching him through binoculars, would have the little craft hauled back onto the *Shark* before submerging and putting out to open sea again. The Chinese would find no evidence to indicate that anyone had been landed in the area.

On the water distances were deceptive, and this stage of the journey that had begun five years earlier seemed endless. Beyond the concrete-reinforced reefs that hid the main harbor from sight a military band was playing, and Larry heard an occasional burst of brassy music. He recognized two of the songs, marches that the tough, battle-scarred veterans of Red dictator Mao Tse-tung's wars had bel-

13

lowed defiantly when they had lived in caves and fought the established government of the Nationalists in the agonizing era of civil strife before World War II.

Suddenly Larry became aware of the faint but distinct sound of another motor. He peered off into the darkness on his starboard side, and after a few moments was able to make out the outlines of an old-fashioned Chinese junk, her hull gracefully rounded, her aft deck high above the waterline, her multicolored sails flapping. But this was no ordinary junk that depended on sails and wind for power. Apparently she was equipped with a diesel engine, and cut swiftly through the water.

She seemed to be heading in Larry's general direction, and he was afraid that she might be a patrol ship operated by the Tientsin harbor militia. Perhaps something suspicious had been noted, and she was coming to investigate.

Using an aluminum oar painted dark green as a rudder, he immediately steered toward the sheltering rocks of the natural reef off to his port side. Although his knowledge of the sea was limited, he had been taught what to do in just such an emergency and reacted at once. If the men on the junk were searching for an intruder he and his little boat would be at least partly visible against a background of the twenty-foot-high dark rocks, so he headed around their point to the water beyond them, hoping to put them between him and his possible pursuers.

Then he felt a wave of panic. The nylon line, many hundreds of yards long, that still bound him to the *Shark* might become fouled in the blades of the junk's motor. If that should happen the harbor militiamen might catch sight of the submarine's camouflaged sail at the outer side of the harbor. An alarm would be given and the Chinese would discover that an American warship had crept into the waters off Tientsin.

Larry reached down to his heel, tapped on it, and drew his knife. He would cut the line rather than risk placing Captain Richards and the crew of the *Shark* in jeopardy. But he paused with his hand only a few inches from the rapidly uncoiling line. His own chances of escaping detection would be severely decreased if he cut the line, as it would be difficult for him to dispose of the rubber boat and outboard motor. In case of absolute necessity he would sink it, as he had been taught, but an oil slick might rise to the surface or a small part might come loose and float. If the craft — or any portion of it — should be found there was a chance that the authorities would suspect that an alien agent had been landed, making his job all the more difficult.

He played out an extra hundred yards of the line and held his breath as the junk cut

15

between him and the submarine. He began to perspire heavily, even though the night was bitterly cold. Then the junk glided on, the blades of her motor still purring smoothly. The weight of the waterlogged line had hauled it deep beneath the surface of the sea, and the junk had passed over it.

As nearly as he could guess, the men on board suspected no unusual activity. If they were harbor militia they were simply making a routine inspection and had seen nothing out of the ordinary.

Almost too late Larry became aware of a fresh danger. His fragile boat was heading straight toward the ugly reef, and he could make out the shapes of jagged rocks submerged beneath the surface. Contact with just one of those rocks would tear great holes in the rubber hull and sink the little boat.

He veered off, avoided one rock by inches and grazed another before he could maneuver into open water again. Safe now, he strained for the sound of the junk's motor, but could hear nothing. The vessel had vanished into the night, so he started toward the shore again.

A quick look at the luminous dial of his wristwatch made him uneasy. The incident had delayed him for almost a quarter of an hour, and every additional second that the submarine was forced to wait, the risk of discovery became greater. But his outboard was going at full speed, and he tried to curb his tension.

Another ten minutes passed before Larry finally heard the gentle slap-slap of water against smooth stones. He knew that directly ahead was the five-hundred-year-old seawall built by the slaves of a mighty Chinese emperor. The end of his journey was at hand.

He could no longer make out even the haziest outline of the *Shark*'s sail, and was certain that he couldn't be seen from the ship either. But the intelligence officers who had planned the operation had thought of this possibility. Larry opened a flap on the bottom of the rubber boat and drew out an infrared light shaped like a pencil. Leaping up onto the seawall, he snapped on the light and swung it in a wide arc, very slowly and deliberately, three times.

Since Captain Richards' binoculars were fitted with an infrared sighting device, the skipper of the *Shark* would know that Larry had landed safely. Again Larry waited, picturing the scene on board the submarine as the members of the crew hauled in the nylon line. Finally the line became taut, and the rubber boat began to move, silently and seemingly under its own power.

At the last possible moment Larry remembered that he was still clutching the infrared light. He squinted, lobbed it, and heaved a sigh of relief when he heard a slight thud as it landed inside the boat. A moment later the craft disappeared from sight, and again Larry checked his watch. Trusted members of the crew had practiced this part of the operation repeatedly. So he knew that it would take them three and a half minutes to haul the boat out to the *Shark,* two minutes to prepare for submersion, and another two to get under way.

Those seven and a half minutes were the longest of his life. He waited an extra thirty seconds and then assumed that the *Shark* had vanished beneath the surface of the water and was threading toward the safety of the open sea.

He had penetrated the Bamboo Curtain successfully; now the time had come for him to look after himself.

He began to walk rapidly past the concrete warehouses, their doors barred and locked to prevent looting. Gradually moving away from the waterfront, he went up one deserted street and down another as he headed toward the scene of the New Year ceremonies.

2

IN ALL THE YEARS Larry had lived in China, first as the schoolboy son of an American missionary, and then in his late teens as an interpreter for the U. S. Army Intelligence during the closing years of World War II, he had never liked Tientsin. Peking had always reminded him of a grand old lady, still showing strong traces of the glittering pomp she once had known as the capital of a centuries-old empire. Shanghai was sophisticated, as cosmopolitan and exciting as New York, London, or Paris. Canton was typical of the south, a sprawling giant where people had always been more important than industry and progress.

But Tientsin was a rude, bustling port, a place where even the polite, considerate men and women from other parts of China forgot their good manners. Crowds were surly, everyone shoved, and nobody bothered to ask anyone else's pardon. Tientsin hadn't changed.

Battling his way through the mob that overflowed the high-domed, glass-roofed railroad station, Larry suddenly remembered something that Sue Chang had said a short time before they had been married.

"In Tientsin," she had told him, "never apologize when you collide with someone. He'll take it as a sign of weakness, and will knock you down."

In a sense it was a relief to be lost in a jostling, shoving throng. Crowds were anonymous. But, peering over the heads of those around him, Larry soon realized that he would have to part company with the mob. Virtually everyone was heading toward the windows where inexpensive railroad tickets could be bought. However, a small area on the far side of the waiting room, indicated by an inconspicuous sign, was reserved for first-class passengers. A man who had the standing of Richard L. Bliss in the Communist hierarchy would be sure to travel first class, and Larry knew he would stand out more if he tried to hide himself in the crowd.

He elbowed his way toward the first-class section and at last stood in the clear. A metallic voice was broadcasting a newscast through highly amplified loudspeakers, denouncing the "imperialist American warmongers" in bitter terms and attacking China's former ally, Soviet Russia, too. Ordinarily Larry would have spent a few minutes listening, but a quick glance down at his feet told him that he faced a minor crisis which could become very large and dangerous unless he did something about it.

His boots were caked with dried mud. Obviously they had become dirty when he had been making his way through the waterfront warehouse area to the heart of the city. Equally obvious was the need to clean them at once. Richard L. Bliss, deputy director of the Special Ministry, the man in charge of all Red Chinese espionage activities in the United States and Canada, was too high-ranking an official to appear publicly in dirty shoes.

Larry headed toward the first-class washroom, found it empty, and there removed the evidence from his boots. He was relieved to discover that there was no shortage of paper towels in the country and, still cautious, he moved toward a toilet, intending to flush the mud-smeared sheets down the drain. At that moment an infantry major stalked into the washroom.

His uniform was plain, and he wore no decorations on his tunic. His only insignia of rank appeared on his cap. But his arrogant expression indicated that he was a professional soldier, a member of the class that was contemptuous of all civilians. He stood for a moment, staring at Larry, his eyes hard and suspicious.

There was only a split second in which to make a decision. Larry still held the dirty sheets of paper toweling in his hand, and wanted to be rid of them. But he knew that if he carried out his original intention he would succeed only in calling more attention to himself, so he dropped the sheets into a wooden bin, bowed politely, and forced himself to stroll toward a basin to wash his hands.

He deliberately refrained from looking up, and by the time he was clean again, the major had gone. Then, presentable at last, he reentered the waiting room, where he would speak to someone for the first time since being smuggled into the country.

The young woman behind the ticket counter had blue-black hair, worn in a shoulder-length bob. Her figure was concealed under a thick ill-fitting tunic of padded cotton.

Speaking a faultless Mandarin, the dialect Bliss always used, Larry requested a sleeping compartment on the late-night train to Peking. The girl shuffled through his identity papers, then thrust them brusquely across the counter toward him. "Surely you should know, Comrade Bliss," she said in the harsh northern dialect of Hopeh Province, "that in the People's Democracy all first-class compartments must be reserved three months in advance."

Larry promptly replied in the same tongue. "Surely you know, comrade," he retorted, "that the business of Chou En-lai does not wait three months."

The mention of Red China's premier, a member of the ruling presidium and a lifelong associate of dictator Mao Tse-tung, produced a change in the young woman's attitude. She gazed at Larry for a long moment and then burst into laughter.

"Not another," she said, and laughed again.

"I'm afraid I don't appreciate your humor, comrade." Larry smiled too, but remained tense.

"If I were given one hundred yuan every time someone tells me he's transacting business for Chou En-lai, I'd soon be wealthy enough to take a holiday at one of the seaside resorts in the south."

During pre-Communist days bribery had been a part of every business dealing in impoverished China. Larry had been instructed to offer private funds whenever necessary, but he wasn't certain that his teachers had known what they were talking about. The Tientsin railroad station was many thousands of miles from the intelligence training camp, and the young woman behind the counter might be extremely insulted if he tried to bribe her. What

23

was worse, she could cause trouble for him if she reported him, as it was against the law now to give or take bribes.

He decided to probe the subject. "One hundred yuan doesn't buy much these days."

The girl's eyes became guarded. "It buys very little. I would need three hundred for the *cheongsam* I'd need on my holiday."

A *cheongsam*, Larry knew, was the traditional high-necked, slit-skirted dress that had been so popular in China until it had been replaced by the semi-uniform that people of both sexes now wore. One way to discourage their use by women was to place an exorbitant price on them.

"A *cheongsam* of pure silk would cost even more."

"Four hundred and fifty yuan," the girl replied.

Larry took his wallet from his pocket and counted out four hundred and fifty yuan in the slick-feeling paper bills the Chinese used. He casually placed the money on the counter and left it a few inches from his hand as he inquired politely, "And the price of a sleeping compartment to Peking?"

"Ninety yuan for a private room." The girl picked up a form and, copying data from Larry's false identity card, began to write rapidly.

He placed a one-hundred-yuan note on the counter beside the other money.

The girl finished making out the form, which she carefully punched and stamped. Scooping up the money with a discreetly practiced hand, she handed him ten yuan in coins. "Your change, Comrade Bliss."

They exchanged bows, and Larry was careful not to smile. The slightest sign of condescension would make the young woman his enemy.

"I wish you a safe journey and a pleasant night's rest," she said.

"Thanks to you, comrade, I'm sure I shall enjoy both."

Larry had thought no one had witnessed the exchange, but as he turned away from the counter a porter materialized at his side, took his light canvas bag, and headed toward the platform where the Peking Express was waiting.

Following him, Larry was faintly amused, but felt sad too. The government boasted that China was a classless society, that there were no more servants. But it seemed that there were always people to wait on officials who were important enough.

As they walked down the platform past railroad coaches that were completely barren except for a long double bench down the middle of the car Larry realized that China was unchanged in other ways too. Scores of men, women, and even small children were crammed into the coaches, most of them standing, with scarcely room to turn around. They would press close together in the badly ventilated car, patiently waiting until the train started on its journey in the small hours of the morning. Then, lurching and swaying, they would be carried to Peking, where they would disembark meekly after spending a sleepless night on their feet.

The first-class dining and sleeping cars offered a sharp contrast. Lamps gleamed on tables set with spotless linen; silverware was burnished; and the beds, which Larry glimpsed through the windows, looked luxuriously inviting. As he had expected, the porter accepted a tip from him. Then the car attendant went through his papers and found everything in order.

The attendant bowed him into his room, and as Larry closed and locked the door behind him he sighed deeply. So far his luck had been good — almost too good.

He jumped suddenly as the strains of the Communist anthem, the *Internationale,* almost broke his eardrums. A full orchestra was playing the song, and as the last notes died away a deep male voice said, "Comrades, for the coming hours, the Ministry of Education and Englightenment brings you the news of the world."

Larry didn't know whether to laugh or become annoyed. Directly over the head of his bed was a loudspeaker, and a brief examination confirmed his guess that there was no way he could shut off the instrument. It would be impossible for him to sleep with the propaganda blaring.

Curbing his irritation, he pondered briefly. How would Bliss handle such a situation? Not even a misguided zealot would go to bed with a newscaster's voice amplified so loudly that the walls of the compartment seemed to shake.

A buzzer ring brought the attendant to the door. "Something seems to be wrong with my radio," Larry said blandly. "I believe that only a minor repair is necessary. And I wonder if you could take care of it for me."

The attendant's expression remained unchanged as he produced a ring of keys, inserted one into the panel at the front of the speaker, and swung it open. He pulled out a single wire, the voice ceased abruptly, and there was a blessed silence in the compartment. It was clear from the attendant's attitude and skill that he had performed this same task many times for other first-class passengers.

No further words were exchanged, but

27

Larry slipped a folded bill into the man's hand as the attendant bowed himself out.

Larry double-locked and bolted the door, undressed, and, as a final precaution, placed his Chinese automatic under his pillow as he climbed into bed. He expected no trouble before reaching Peking, but a man in his position couldn't afford to take chances.

Stretching out in the warm bed, he allowed his mind to go blank for a few minutes as he enjoyed the respite from the tensions of the long day. Then he snapped off the overhead light and, scarcely aware of what he was doing, began to review the events that had brought him so far from home, under such bizarre circumstances. . . .

The editors of *Global News* had long called Larry a walking encyclopedia on China. So, in 1949, they sent him to Hong Kong as their chief Far Eastern correspondent. There, by chance, he encountered Sue Chang, whom he had known during the war, and six months later they were married.

But Larry's civilian career was short. When the Korean War erupted he was recalled to military duty as a member of a special intelligence team working under his former superior, Major General Howard Hopkins. Sue went to live on the farm at Stony Ridge, Vermont, that he had inherited from his parents.

And when Larry was released from the army after two years, with the rank of lieutenant colonel, Sue was waiting for him with David, their son.

The years that followed were the happiest Larry had ever known. He bought the local newspaper in Stony Ridge and soon became a respected member of the community. Sue was popular with everyone in town, and David, a bright boy, stood second in his class and had the hottest Little League bat in the county. He was proudly conscious of his Eurasian heritage, and spoke Chinese soon after he learned English. By the time he was ten he spoke two Chinese dialects, Mandarin and Hopeh, without an accent.

That same year Larry received an offer that seemed at the time to be a golden opportunity. The United States was becoming increasingly involved in South Vietnam, and *Global News,* his former employers, asked him to go to Saigon for several months to prepare a series of articles on the situation there, as he saw it.

Larry gasped at the size of the fee. "I'm tempted," he said. "But I'll be honest with you. When I came home from Korea I promised my wife I'd never be separated from her and our son for more than four weeks. I can't break my word to her."

"Take your family with you," the *Global News* editor told him. "We want you badly for this assignment, so we'll pay their expenses too."

Sue was elated. She and Larry had many friends in Hong Kong, and could visit them. Here too was an unexpected chance for David to pay a long visit to the Orient — and practice speaking Chinese.

The family talked it over for several days and finally decided that they would make the trip. They would fly to Hong Kong, and after spending a few days there Larry would go on to Saigon. There, in three or four weeks, Sue and David would join him. He was reluctant to let them stay too long in the war-torn city, so they agreed that Sue and David would return to Hong Kong and that Larry would pick them up there when he completed his assignment.

Everything went according to plan. David was fascinated by what he saw in Hong Kong, and by the time Larry left for Saigon, his son was already at ease with a half-dozen boys his own age. Less than a month later, when he and Sue joined Larry, David knew all the current slang in the Hopeh dialect.

The family's stay in Saigon was somewhat less successful, and Larry privately was relieved when his wife and son went back to Hong Kong. Saigon, where assassins roamed the streets at night and terrorists threw plastic bombs into cafés and automobiles in broad daylight, was no place for a quiet house-wife and a ten-year-old boy.

The nightmare began just four days before Larry was scheduled to leave Saigon. He was in his hotel room, dressing for the day, when the telephone rang, and he heard the voice of a high-ranking official whom he knew at the United States consulate in Hong Kong.

"Larry," his friend said, "the only way I know to break the news to you is to give it to you straight. Your wife is dead and your son has vanished."

Less than an hour later Larry was on board a plane bound for the little British crown colony off the Chinese mainland. There he was greeted by a large group of officials, including a deputy police commissioner, a former brig-adier in the British army who had been trained for his present post by Scotland Yard.

"Our tests," said the brigadier, "indicate beyond all doubt that Mrs. Heddon was mur-dered in her hotel suite. Apparently she re-sisted one or more intruders who entered dur-ing the night, and they killed her."

Larry could only stare at him. "Why did they do it? Sue had no enemies, and I don't believe I have any either."

"We're trying to find out, Mr. Heddon. At the moment all I can tell you is that the motive certainly wasn't robbery. None of your wife's belongings was touched. We're questioning hotel employees and making an investigation of other guests at the hotel."

Larry was still in a state of shock. "Have you — found David?"

The brigadier shook his head. "He's disappeared without a trace."

"But I don't understand why anyone would want to kidnap him. I can't afford to pay a large ransom."

"A squad of my best men is working on the case. We'll let you know when we have some leads."

The Hong Kong detectives came up with no clues, and the mystery of David's disappearance deepened. Larry launched an investigation of his own, too, but learned nothing. His friends in the Chinese community had no helpful information, and members of the British and foreign colonies were equally blank.

All that could be said with any degree of certainty was that someone — perhaps one man, more probably several — had climbed up the trellis on the outer wall of the hotel and had entered the suite via the balcony. The rest was conjecture. The brigadier believed, and Larry was inclined to agree with him, that Sue had lost her life trying to prevent her son from being kidnapped.

For week after weary week Larry pursued leads and clues that proved to be false, and followed hunches that led nowhere. When his funds ran low he forced himself to go to work, and spent several hours each day writing the series of articles commissioned by *Global News*.

One evening the brigadier invited him to dinner and gently urged him to go home. "Mr. Heddon," he said, "trying to solve a crime in Hong Kong is like trying to find the proverbial needle in the proverbial haystack. Chinese refugees by the tens of thousands cross the border every year."

Larry nodded. He had visited the nearby Portuguese colony of Macao for ten days, but had failed to uncover any information on David's whereabouts there either. "I realize it may be hopeless," he said, "but I've got to keep trying."

The weeks stretched into months. Larry employed every investigative technique that he had learned in military intelligence, but to no avail. The earth appeared to have swallowed up David, without reason.

Then, after five long dreary months, came a night Larry would never forget. He had spent the evening at a waterfront café, wasting his time tracking down a clue that had led nowhere. It was very late when he started back to his hotel, and there were no taxis, rickshaws, or pedicabs in sight, so he decided to walk.

Suddenly a short man with the slender build

33

of the southern Chinese darted out of a deserted alleyway. Larry reached for the pistol he now carried at all times.

"You want to find out about your boy?" the man asked in the Cantonese dialect. "Come with me."

Larry looked up and down the dark street, but no policeman was in sight, nor was anyone else. He had no choice, even though he knew he might be the intended victim of a trick. Some refugees were so poor — and so desperate — that they would not hesitate to kill a man for the money he carried in his wallet and the clothes on his back.

There was no conversation as Larry accompanied his guide down twisting alleyways and narrow streets to the waterfront. There another man awaited them in a small rowboat and transported them to a dilapidated junk, a vessel that resembled scores of other houseboats anchored near it. Larry observed everything closely, trying to remember each detail and imprint the precise location of the junk on his mind.

His guides knew what he was doing, but neither commented until they reached the junk, boarded it, and walked into a foul-smelling cabin. Then the Cantonese said quietly, "You carry a weapon, Mr. Heddon. Please surrender it to me. It will be returned to you later."

Larry realized that the risk was great, but

the man knew his name, so there was at least a slim chance that the offer of information about David was legitimate. Silently he handed the Cantonese his pistol.

"Now," the man said, "we must blindfold you before we continue our short journey."

Larry suffered misgivings as he allowed a strip of cloth to be tied over his eyes. Then he was led back to the rowboat. As nearly as he could judge, he spent another quarter of an hour or more in it before he was helped onto the deck of another vessel and taken below.

His captors seated him in a chair and, ignoring his protests, tied his hands securely behind his back. Suddenly his blindfold was removed, and he blinked in the unaccustomed glare of two strong kerosene lamps. The door closed, and Larry was alone.

He knew, as he looked around, that this was no ordinary junk. The cabin was comfortably furnished with chairs and tables; several hand-painted silk screens hid the ugly bulkheads; and the deck beneath his feet was covered with a thick rug. A glazed porcelain cup stood on a table beside him, and he was surprised to see that it was filled with American cigarettes.

The door opened and a fair-skinned blond man came into the cabin. He was wearing expensively tailored Chinese clothes, and took care not to let his trousers become wrinkled as he lowered himself into a chair opposite Larry.

"Well, Heddon," he said, speaking English with an American accent, "you and I have been chasing each other on a treadmill for a long time. Or maybe it's been a merry-go-round. I'm never quite sure."

"I've been on my own private merry-go-round," Larry said dryly.

"Call it whatever you please, but you've been too active for our tastes. You stirred up the police too much. I've had to wait until things quieted down before having this little chat with you."

Larry waited, saying nothing.

"You surprised me. You're an old hand in our business, and you certainly should have learned long before now that you let the mud settle at the bottom so you can see the fish."

"Who in blazes are you?"

"I've been in your files for years, just as you've been in mine. My name is Bliss, Richard L. Bliss."

Larry stiffened. Everyone in the United States who read newspapers, listened to radios, or watched television was familiar with the case of Bliss, the brilliant graduate of an Ivy League college who had defected from his important government position to join the Red Chinese. Larry himself knew a great deal more about the man. Bliss had become an executive in the Chinese intelligence apparatus, and Larry had spent many long and fruitless hours during the Korean War questioning captured espionage agents who had been working under Bliss's supervision.

The man grinned amiably. "I thought you'd be surprised." He studied Larry, and his smile broadened. "It's actually true."

"What is?"

"You and I look alike. Nobody would mistake us for brothers, but we might be cousins."

"You haven't gone through a lot of elaborate hocus-pocus to tell me that our eyes are t' same color." Larry's voice was harsh. "Wh re is my son?"

"All in good time, Heddon. I can appreciate your impatience, and although I'm a bachelor myself, I sympathize with your concern for the boy."

"Thanks a heap, but spare me your tender sentiments."

Bliss leaned forward in his chair. "There's one thing I'd like to get straight. I meant you no personal harm. Take my word or reject it, that's the way it was."

"Meaning?"

Bliss's voice became a shade gentler. "Mrs. Heddon. I had to depend on another department for that part of the job. As usual, they were too anxious. And clumsy."

Larry had to exert all his self-control. Probably the man's apology was sincere enough, but Sue's death —savage and unnecessary — was still a raw wound.

"Of all people, you can appreciate the spot I'm in, Colonel Heddon."

Larry hadn't been addressed as "Colonel" in a long time.

"I need you," the turncoat said bluntly. "There are some big holes in our organization. We need a man with your talents to fill the biggest of them."

"You flatter me."

"You're a patriot, of course. Every man to his own poison. Anyway, we knew you needed some inducements to loosen up your thinking. My front office has assigned me to persuade you to join us. It's that simple. I'm prepared to make you an offer. If you'll provide us regularly with certain information we seek — information easily available to you because you're trusted by American intelligence — we'll return your son to you unharmed. After you've done several jobs for us, to be sure, and have been so thoroughly compromised that you can't turn on us without sending yourself to prison for a long term."

At last it was all clear. David was being held as a hostage in order to force Larry to become a Chinese espionage agent. And Sue's tragic death had been simply an accident.

Every word had to be weighed with care.

"How do I know," Larry asked, "that this isn't a hoax? How do I know my son hasn't been killed?"

"Sensible questions that I'm prepared to answer." Bliss reached into a tunic pocket.

Larry found himself staring at a snapshot of David in Chinese padded tunic and trousers. He had grown taller in recent months, his face was thinner, and his eyes were no longer those of a little boy. Then Bliss turned over the picture, and on the back was an inscription in David's hand. "Dear Daddy," he had written, "I'm okay. Love, David."

Larry made a supreme effort to keep a grip on himself. "I'm still listening," he said gruffly.

"Obviously this isn't a matter you can decide on the spur of the moment. Leave Hong Kong. Go home to the United States and think things over. In due time we will get in touch with you."

Larry's throat felt painfully dry. "What will happen to David if I refuse to work for you?"

Bliss shrugged indifferently. Then, moving very quickly, he stood and left the cabin.

Even now, five years later, Larry felt hot, then cold, as he recalled that interview. Unable to sleep, he continued to stare up at the ceiling of the train that would soon be under way taking him to Peking — and a possible reunion

39

with David. After all this time the miracle seemed too good to be true.

Patrol boats of the Hong Kong police department scoured the harbor, but the deisel-operated junk was gone. And Larry was unable to identify the other junk on which he had first been blindfolded, then set free. At least a dozen seemed to fit its description, but large numbers of refugees were crowded onto each of them. It was impossible to determine whether people had been moved off, then returned to one of them. So many of the refugees had relatives still in China that they could be cowed into obeying the Red authorities. The brigadier said there was no way of finding out whether the occupants of one or another junk had cooperated with the Communists the previous night. Even if a frightened refugee had been persuaded to tell the truth, it was unlikely that he could give the authorities any information about the elusive diesel-engined junk. Bliss wasn't the sort to take obvious risks.

Twenty-four hours later Larry flew home to the United States, asking himself the same question again and again: Should he become a traitor to his country in order to have his son returned to him?

In a sense he had already given his answer when he had gone straight to the Hong Kong police. He had no guarantee that David would actually be set free if he became a Chinese espionage agent. Even more important, he wouldn't be able to live with himself, nor would David respect him. Larry flew straight to Washington.

"I want to beat them at their own game," he told Howard Hopkins, now a lieutenant general and one of the heads of a large and secret government intelligence agency. "Let me pretend to go along with Bliss. I'll feed him false information, and—"

"That won't work," General Hopkins told him. "Bliss is too clever, and if you try to fool him he's likely to have your son killed."

"Then smuggle me into China, and I'll find some way to get David out!"

"Now you're being unrealistic, Larry. We've had the devil's own time setting up a small organization in China. And you know as well as I do that it can't be used for the purpose of helping private American citizens, no matter how great the individual's need. All I can do is promise that I'll try to have our people find out what's become of your son. There's literally nothing else I can do for you."

A heartbroken Larry returned to Stony Ridge. A few weeks later he received — and ignored — a letter from Bliss asking him to write to a Hong Kong post-office-box address.

That was his answer to the Chinese. And two and a half long years passed before he received a telephone call from General Hopkins. "Your son is alive and well," the general told him. "The word has just been passed out to us. It's all we know."

Life had never been so bleak.

More than four years after David had been kidnapped Larry was unexpectedly summoned to Washington, where General Hopkins greeted him with a deceptive surface calm. "Do you still want to go to China?"

"Yes, if David is alive."

"He is, although that's beside the point. Larry, we need you. There's a job only you can do for us."

Larry scowled.

"We've learned a great deal in this past year. Richard Bliss has been put in charge of a new espionage apparatus that's working out of San Francisco. We suspect he may be using residents of Chinatown — it has the largest Chinese population in the United States, and Red agents would be relatively inconspicuous there. We need their names — and any other data available on them."

Larry shook his head. "General, you're asking for a slice of the moon."

"Maybe so. But we think you're just the fellow who can bring it back to us."

42

"Why me?"

"Because your qualifications are unique. Most of our operatives over there are Orientals, Nationalist Chinese from Taiwan posing as Reds. For this job we need a blue-eyed American. You started me thinking when you told me you and Bliss have something of a physical resemblance."

"Hold on!"

"Let me finish, Larry. You've met Bliss, so you have at least some idea of his personality and mannerisms. You're a trained intelligence officer who can get a job done. You're thoroughly familiar with China, and you speak the language like a native. I doubt if there's another American alive with your qualifications."

"I'm listening," Larry said sourly, "but I'm not impressed."

"We've learned Bliss's complete personal setup. We want to send you in — to impersonate him. Somewhere, either in his apartment or his office — probably his office — you'll have to pick up clues. I wouldn't think he'd keep top-secret data on his San Francisco operation kicking around in the open. We know there's a records room for secret documents in the headquarters where he has his office. You'll find the whole story there, if nowhere else."

"As easy as all that, huh? What do I do about Bliss himself, strangle him?" The sarcasm in Larry's voice was heavy.

"Either that or shoot him, I presume," General Hopkins replied quietly. "He lives alone and rarely entertains visitors. We've learned that he sees something of a woman, but I'll admit we know nothing about her. In any case, she doesn't go to his apartment."

"You seriously want me to impersonate him? There must be hundreds of people who'd spot me as an impostor in a minute!"

"Not by the time our plastic surgeons and preparation teams are finished with you. You'll look like his identical twin, and you'll be stuffed full of information on him."

"There's a litt' matter of positive identification called fingerprints." Larry was still caustic.

"One of the boys brought that up at staff meeting. The Chinese system of storing personal data is very convenient for this purpose. Bliss's prints, photo, and so forth are kept in a special personnel file in the same Peking headquarters building. We'll show you fairly complete diagrams of the place that one of our operatives made. You can substitute your prints for those of Bliss, which might be difficult, I'll admit. Or you can destroy the whole card."

Larry glared across the desk. "If your people can get you diagrams of an intelligence headquarters building in Peking why can't

44

they steal the information you want on the San Francisco operations pool?"

"Because" General Hopkins said patiently, "only Bliss has access to that information. And only you are capable of impersonating him."

"You have all the answers except one, General. You're being coy about David."

"Your son is a student at a boarding school in a Peking suburb. The sons of prominent Red officials are sent there. Bliss has become his guardian, more or less, and from what we gather through one of our men, apparently intends to use him as an agent when he's a little older. A boy of Eurasian parentage who speaks perfect English and perfect Chinese can be very useful to an espionage organization."

"Of course." Larry was silent for a moment. "How thoroughly has David been indoctrinated?"

The general met his gaze. "I wish I could tell you, but I honestly don't know. That's a problem you'll have to handle in your own way when you get over there." He leaned forward, tapping a miniature saber letter opener to emphasize his words. "You've wanted us to smuggle you into China, and I'm giving you the chance. But there are ground rules you'll have to observe. Anything you do to rescue your son will be your own affair. I can't risk the lives

45

of the few people we have there to help him. From where we sit, your mission for us comes first."

Larry realized that the general was doing everything possible to help him, and that the conditions were more than fair. Suddenly he sighed. "I haven't seen David in a very long time." He was speaking to himself.

"Then you'll accept?"

Larry shrugged. "Why not? There's a lot to gain, and nothing to lose except a life that doesn't mean much to me any more."

General Hopkins stood and shook his hand.

The sound of a piercing, high-pitched whistle cut through the night, and the Tientsin–Peking Express moved slowly out of the glass-roofed station, gathering speed as it traveled through the city and headed westward across the ancient rugged hills of northern China. Larry closed his eyes and felt curiously at peace with himself. After six months of the most intensive preparations that the intelligence agencies of the United States had been able to devise he was on the last lap of his long journey to the capital of Red China.

3

PEKING ITSELF was basically unchanged, although the industrial suburbs had expanded enormously. Here and there Larry saw rows of ugly concrete apartment houses that had risen since he had last visited the city, and there were also some huge new office buildings to accommodate the officials of the mammoth bureaucratic Communist government. Riding in the bucketlike seat of a pedicab in front of the cycling driver, Larry felt a positive sense of pleasure as he gazed at some of the most handsome buildings on earth, reminders of China's proud heritage. The great metropolis designed by Kublai Khan and improved by the rulers of the later Ming and Manchu dynasties stood permanent and immortal.

Off to the west in the hills he caught glimpses of the Great Wall, built on crests of the four-thousand-foot-high peaks. For close to three thousand years that shield had stood

47

between the Chinese capital and the savage nomads of Manchuria. The palaces of the Inner City, or Forbidden City, were intact too, their pagoda roofs curving gracefully, the multicolored buildings serene behind sturdy pillars, as was the Porcelain Pagoda with its seven lovely, intricately fashioned terraces. Through the long centuries these structures had known many inhabitants and had outlasted them all.

The pedicab turned onto the gracious Imperial Road, now called Lenin Boulevard, and, after passing through the massive Ch'ien Men Gate, rolled through heavy traffic. Larry smiled to himself when he saw a sign on the handsome Temple of Heaven, reminding the city's residents that it was now called the Haven of Workers' Solidarity. He resisted the temptation to say something about the renowned Bell Tower, which in ages past had rung a nightly curfew for the citizens. The new rulers had shown the good sense not to change its name, but Larry knew the driver probably wouldn't appreciate the humor of a comment to that effect.

The Legation Quarter, famous since it had withstood the siege of imperial troops in the Boxer Rebellion of 1900, was still imposing. Foreign flags fluttered from masts above many of the embassies, but Larry felt a quick pang when he saw that the United States legation was now being used as an office building by the Chinese government. The sight served as a reminder that he was not just an alien here, that Americans were regarded as China's enemies.

The people were changed far more than their city. Everywhere men, women, and even children wore padded tunics and trousers of faded blue or dull gray. Watching them as they trudged down the streets or rode their bicycles, their faces set and expressionless, Larry was reminded of a vast colony of hard-working, humorless ants. No one, he saw, paid attention to the newscasts blaring from loudspeakers set up at the major intersections.

The pedicab turned into Little Flower Lane, now called Steel Workers Street, and Larry tensed. In a few moments he would arrive at Bliss's apartment. Reaching inside his tunic, he removed the safety catch from his automatic and made certain that the silencer attachment was securely in place.

The cab drew to a halt, and as Larry paid the driver he saw a lean, gray-haired woman standing on the stoop of the three-story building, looking at him. According to descriptions with which he had been furnished, he guessed that this was "his" landlady.

So far, everything was going as planned.

By this time of morning Bliss would be at his office, and there would be ample time to become familiar with the apartment, wait for the man, and shoot him when he returned home at the end of the day. Only one problem remained half solved. No one had known quite what to do with Bliss's body, but a panel of intelligence experts attending the Pennsylvania briefings had agreed that it would be best to hide the corpse in a closet. Larry would have to complete his mission within a very short time, and as Bliss entertained no visitors, a week or two might pass before anyone discovered the body.

The person most likely to find it would be the landlady, and Larry looked at her obliquely. She seemed harmless enough, but he knew better. The custodians of virtually all residences in China were devoted Communists who were under strict instructions to keep watch on their tenants, record the visits of unusual or suspicious guests, and when requested, inspect incoming mail.

The woman's reaction would be critical. If she knew he was an imposter his mission would come to an abrupt end before it even began.

"Good morning, Mrs. Peng," Larry said with pretended casualness, taking care to speak Mandarin, as Bliss always did.

The woman replied in the Hopeh dialect.

"Welcome home, Comrade Bliss. Did you have a pleasant journey?"

Larry felt a sense of almost overwhelming relief. Apparently Bliss had been out of the city, so there could be no immediate encounter with him. One complication was removed — for the present. "I make so many trips that one is like another," he said.

The woman seemed inclined to chat. "I pushed your mail under your door."

"Thank you."

"There was nothing important. Just the usual."

Larry smiled, but made no comment. However, he continued to linger on the stoop.

"I didn't expect you so soon," Mrs. Peng said, and the remark sounded almost like an accusation.

Larry concealed his mounting excitement. Here was an unexpected chance to learn something of real value. "When did you think I'd be coming home?"

She sniffed disdainfully. "You paid your rent for three months in advance!"

This was beginning to sound better and better. Perhaps he could perform his entire mission and leave before Bliss returned. "I hope," he said deliberately, "that there's enough canned food in my apartment for breakfast. I've had no time to buy fresh food this morning."

The landlady, who had no intention of sharing her own rationed supplies, hastily preceded him into the building. "Glory to Comrade Mao," she said.

"And to the People's Republic." Larry started up the stairs as she retreated into her own ground-floor apartment. At the third-floor landing he paused, took a key from a trouser pocket, and, dropping his canvas bag onto the floor, turned the key in the lock. The apartment door creaked open, and the musty odor assured Larry that the place hadn't been used in some time. He closed the door behind him and made a quick tour through the unfamiliar apartment. The living room was unoccupied, as were the bedroom and small kitchen. There were two clothes closets, and he found nothing out of the ordinary in either. Relaxing slightly, he raised several of the bamboo blinds to let in the harsh winter daylight.

Uncertain how long he would remain undisturbed, he made a hasty search of the apartment, beginning with the mail. As Mrs. Peng had indicated, the letters seemed unimportant; most were small bills. One intrigued him, however. In a woman's hand, and written, surprisingly, in English, it was signed by someone who called herself "Laura" and who asked Bliss to telephone her when he returned to Peking. Larry shrugged and put the letter aside. Apparently this was the woman Washington had mentioned to him in passing, but he couldn't concern himself with Bliss's social life. He had the descriptions of too many important people to keep straight and might not be as fortunate the next time as he had been with Mrs. Peng.

Bliss was a neat, methodical man who kept his house in order, Larry conceded. Suits of clothes, including several Western-style outfits, were hanging in straight rows in the closets. Dresser drawers were orderly, shoes were shined, and nothing seemed in need of repair. But something struck Larry as strange. He was repeatedly impressed by the lack of personal touches.

Richard L. Bliss was a colorful man and might even be classified as an eccentric, but his belongings completely failed to reflect his personality. A record player stood in one corner of the living room, but the long-playing records in the cabinet beside it were surprisingly banal. The collection consisted of Red marches and some propaganda songs. There were no jazz records, no Western classics, and no musical selections from China's rich cultural heritage.

The contents of the bookcase were similarly barren. There were leather-bound copies, in both English and Chinese, of the works of

53

Marx, Lenin, and Mao Tse-tung, and a cheap edition of the *Workers' Encyclopedia* occupied one entire shelf. But there were no novels, no biographies or other works of nonfiction, and only one slender volume of poetry. Bliss, it appeared, had made strenuous efforts to reveal nothing of his personal life or tastes in his apartment.

The desk was the worst disappointment. Larry found a number of Chinese writing brushes, two jars of ink, and several Western-made ball-point pens. There were stacks of inexpensive paper and envelopes, and a box of heavy rag paper that had cost a great deal more. But Bliss had left no notes, no scraps on which he had written anything. Even a small ledger bound in imitation leather contained little of value.

In it was a careful accounting of Bliss's cash expenses over a six-month period. He had paid regular sums to a dry cleaner, a laundry, and a seller of aromatic tea. He had made purchases of food from a grocer and a butcher, but had eaten most of his meals in the "commune," an inexpensive cafeteria that served the government employees who worked in a complex of office buildings. That was a fact Larry already knew.

Only one item was intriguing. There were several entries marked "gasoline." So it was evident that Bliss sometimes had access to an automobile. There were few cars in Red China available to anyone except the highest government officials, and Larry made a mental note to learn more, if he could, about the automobile that Bliss either borrowed or perhaps obtained from a government pool. A car might prove useful at some future date.

The tiny refrigerator in the kitchen was empty, except for several trays of hard-frozen ice cubes. Bliss had obviously left Peking expecting to be away for some time, but hadn't bothered to turn off the current. On a shelf were stacked two or three dozen cans of food, some Chinese products, others coming from Czechoslovakia, with a few tins of Albanian sardines at one side.

The sight of the food reminded Larry that he had eaten nothing except a skimpy breakfast of tea and thin rice cakes on the train. There was so much to be done, quickly, that he hated to waste time on food. But an old military-intelligence maxim crossed his mind: "Eat when you have the opportunity. You don't know when you'll get your next meal."

So he opened a can of meat stew that bore a Nanking label, heated it on a temperamental gas range, and downed it rapidly. It was barely palatable; the meat was stringy and the vegetables were far too soft and unseasoned.

It was something of a relief to finish, then wash and dry the pot, bowl, and spoon he had found in a cupboard.

Still hoping to discover something that would lead him to the list of Bliss's North American agents — assuming that such a document existed — Larry made a more careful search of the apartment. He looked for wall safes behind pictures; he felt the overstuffed furniture and even turned the mattress on the bed. Nowhere could he locate even a scrap connected with Bliss's espionage work.

It was late morning when he finished, and, after putting his bag on an empty closet shelf, he sat down to consider the situation. Under the careful timetable worked out before he had left the United States, he would not go to Bliss's office until late afternoon, when clerks and other low-level employees would leave for the day. According to the original plan, he was to wait at the apartment, dispose of Bliss, and then go to the intelligence headquarters at a time when there would be few people on hand who might want to engage him in conversation.

Bliss's absence from the city gave him an unexpected opportunity. And Larry was eager to seize it: there was nothing to prevent him from going out to the suburb of Pei-ho, where the Sun Yat-sen Academy for Boys was located, to see David.

The sooner he established contact with his son, the better. But he warned himself that, more than ever before in his life, he would need to keep a tight grip on his emotions.

Several personal problems were still unresolved. Should he reveal his true identity to his son? Or might the knowledge, at this juncture, place David in jeopardy? Larry didn't know the answers, but would have to proceed one step at a time, making his decisions as he went along. After a five-year separation David might well be a stranger to him, even a Communist party member.

The day was so cold that Larry took an overcoat and a pair of gloves from the closet, marveling that they fitted so well. The men responsible for this mission had known what they were doing when they had selected an agent approximately the same height and weight as Richard L. Bliss.

The streets were crowded with pedestrians in blue or gray tunics and trousers, office workers hurrying to communes for a lunch of soup and bread. Seeing them, Larry revised his thinking about Peking, which had changed in more ways than he had realized. Before the Red take-over the great city had been gracious, her people charming and polite. Now they were like the citizens of Tientsin. Everyone rushed, jostling each other without apology. Larry,

57

dodging, side-stepping, and occasionally using his elbows, walked the four blocks to a bus stop. The bustling pedestrians overflowed into the streets, calmly defying the few automobile drivers and many pedicab operators to do their worst.

Shivering under the bulky overcoat, Larry waited at the bus stop. It was with a feeling of relief that he boarded the sputtering, battered vehicle that belched great clouds of gas fumes. In another hour he would see David.

4

HEADMASTER WONG of the Sun Yat-sen Academy for Boys reminded Larry of two or three of his own teachers when he had been a schoolboy in China. Sly and self-important, Wong undoubtedly treated his charges strictly, punishing even the slightest infringement of the academy's rules. But he fawned on their parents, his superiors, while trying to establish himself on a pretended basis of equality with them.

"I'm surprised you didn't drive yourself out, Comrade Bliss," he said. "It's a long ride to Pei-ho on that infernal bus."

"I had no valid reason to requisition a car," Larry replied carefully, continuing to stand in the headmaster's spacious office.

Wong's chuckle sounded conspiratorial. "Whenever one's automobile is not in good working order, one finds cause to obey the laws of the state."

59

Larry smiled glacially to put the man in his place. "I am here," he said, "to see the boy, Heddon." Ever since he had learned that David was still alive he had been grateful that his Chinese captors had allowed his son to keep his own name.

Headmaster Wong sobered instantly. "Of course, Comrade Bliss." He walked to his desk, rang a buzzer, and, when an attendant appeared, issued rapid instructions. "If you'll be patient for just a moment or two, Comrade Bliss, he'll be here."

Wong eyed his visitor surreptitiously, realized that Comrade Bliss looked preoccupied, and therefore remained discreetly silent. It wasn't easy, dealing with these powerful men who sent their sons and wards to the academy. Headmasters had been banished to punitive labor camps for no reason anyone had ever been able to figure out.

The silence was heavy and prolonged before a tap sounded at the door.

Larry braced himself, clenching his fists behind his back.

"You may enter!" Wong called sharply.

David walked into the office, halted, and carefully raised his right arm in the Communist salute. "Comrade Bliss," he said respectfully. "Comrade Headmaster."

Larry blinked away the tears that threatened to form in his eyes. David was tall and husky and looked lithe beneath his green school-uniform tunic and trousers. His hair was cut short in the approved academy manner, but his resemblance to his mother was startling. Larry wouldn't have recognized his son's voice, of course, and even in this moment of emotional tension wanted to laugh at himself. During his countless hours of daydreaming he had forgotten that David's voice would have changed by the age of fifteen and that he would now speak in a man's baritone.

"If you would care to hold your discussion here, Comrade Bliss," the headmaster said, "I gladly offer you the use of my office."

Larry had no intention of talking in a room that might contain hidden microphones. "I prefer to stroll outdoors," he replied shortly. "I find the weather bracing."

Wong was not in the least surprised. Most of the men who came here were reluctant to speak freely in the office. "Enjoy your visit," he said with forced joviality, and opened the sliding panel windows that faced the garden.

The ground was frozen hard, and snow lay two or three inches deep on the lawn, but the gravel path was clear, and Larry and David walked in silence down the lane lined with miniature oaks. The silence was oppressive, and Larry cleared his throat. "Well, David," he said, feeling inadequate to the occasion.

The boy seemed startled — or was it merely an uneasiness in the presence of his guardian? Perhaps Bliss didn't call him by his Christian name.

"Have you been behaving yourself?" After rehearsing his opening speeches so many times, Larry spoke mechanically, using gruffness to conceal the huskiness in his voice.

"I was given a 'superior' in mathematics," David replied dutifully.

"Good!" Larry's pleasure was genuine.

"And another in dialectical materialism and Marxist doctrine."

"Do you know your communism?"

"As well as I'll ever know it."

It was a relief to detect a note of surliness in David's voice and manner. Perhaps attempts to indoctrinate him had not succeeded. Certainly he didn't sound like a Red puppet, but it was best to prod a bit more. "What do you think of the course?"

"Only what I'm taught." David was being openly resentful now.

Larry wanted to hug him, but remained stern, still playing the role of Bliss. "You recognize the importance of the training you're getting here?"

"I never forget it. I don't have a chance." The boy kicked at a stone on the path and refused to raise his head.

There was a brief silence before Larry asked, "What else do you have to report?"

"I beat Chen Pei-fang in a wrestling match — Marshal Chen's grandson."

Larry caught more than a hint of pleasure in David's voice. "Oh?"

"I rubbed his nose on the mat until it bled. And when I finally pinned him, I kept him there until he apologized, even though the whole school was cheering for him."

"Did you and Chen Pei-fang quarrel?"

"No. Not exactly."

"What did happen?"

"He called me a dirty American."

Larry's hopes soared. Perhaps, through some miracle, David had kept a pro-Western outlook. "Are you one?"

The boy's face became blank again, but the bleakness of his voice indicated his despair. "I'm nothing."

It was agony for Larry to see his son in torment, torn between the world he had once known and the new life to which he had been forced to adjust. "What do you want to be?"

"I don't care." David turned savagely to the man he thought was Richard L. Bliss. "I'll be fine if I'm left alone. If it will make you happy, send me to that corrective labor camp again this summer. I'd rather go there than act like Chen Pei-fang's number-one houseboy!"

"I've been making other plans for your summer," Larry said quietly.

For an instant David was confused, but his reaction solidified into apprehensive suspicion. "How will you punish me?"

"I won't."

"If Chen Pei-fang has the courage to tell his grandfather what happened, the marshal will be very angry."

Larry decided that the moment had come to start revealing his true identity. "Marshal Chen," he said distinctly, "can drown in the Lake of the Ten Thousand Dragon-Devils, for all I care."

David blinked, and uncertain what to say, remained silent.

"The snow on Bald Peak is just right for skiing this winter," Larry said. "The White Sox played great baseball last season, and the University of Texas had another championship football team."

David stiffened, his eyes narrowing. It was obvious that he thought Bliss was trying to trick him in some way, and he was bracing himself for a blow.

They reached the end of the path, and a screen of ornamental bushes, leafless in the winter, partly hid them from the main academy building. "Ginger," Larry said, "had another litter of puppies a couple of months ago."

64

David threw caution to the winds and became openly defiant. "Brag all you please about how much you know, but your spies must have better things to do than snoop on Ginger!"

"She still likes a scrambled egg occasionally too. The only collie in the world with a taste for soft-scrambled."

"What do you want from me now, Comrade Bliss?" All at once David looked very young and vulnerable.

"Would you believe me if I told you I'm not Bliss?"

The boy recovered his poise and threw up his protective barrier again. "I have a lot of studying to do before our holiday after the solidarity parade, so I'd like to go back to the dormitory, please."

"There are ways of transforming a man into another's image," Larry said. "China isn't the only country on earth with clever intelligence techniques."

David still did not respond. The boy's skepticism was a shell that Larry seemed incapable of penetrating. "There are details I can't reveal, but I swear to you that I'm not Richard L. Bliss!"

David laughed harshly. "Then who are you?"

Larry knew he had to go all the way. "Your father."

The boy's laugh became louder. "If that's true, which it couldn't be, why have you waited so long to come?"

"It's a long story." Larry knew that this sounded lame and weak, but he felt incapable of dealing with his son's hostility. "I hope to take you out of China in the immediate future."

"Where are we going, Comrade Bliss?"

"My name is Larry Heddon, and I intend to take my son home to Stony Ridge, Vermont."

David looked the man up and down, scrutinizing him carefully. Then, dissatisfied, he thrust his hands into his trouser pockets and shook his head.

"Eventually you'll believe me, but in the meantime I can't do much to help you unless you cooperate."

David saw that the man was serious, and his cynicism was tempered by a strange, unsettled feeling. "Now you'll tell me what you want me to do."

Larry guessed that Bliss sometimes deliberately confused the boy. "I'm not sure what our next step will be. Everything depends on certain developments that — have nothing to do with you. Are you familiar with Bliss's apartment?"

"You know I've been there many times, Comrade Bliss!"

"When is the parade you mentioned?"

"On Peace and World Friendship Day, of course. The day after tomorrow."

"And you're parading?"

"The whole academy marches."

"At what time will you be finished?"

"I don't know. Around noon, I suppose."

"And then you'll have a holiday?"

"For a few hours."

"All right. Come to the apartment as soon as you're free." Larry's mind was working swiftly. He would have less than forty-eight hours in which to carry out the plans his superiors in Washington had made for him, but he knew he couldn't afford to take much longer than that in any event. With luck, he would have acquired the information that Washington so badly wanted regarding the San Francisco espionage center. Without it, he might well be dead. Either way, he didn't want David involved in a delicate and hazardous operation.

"I'll meet you as soon after noon as you can get there," he continued. "If I'm not there, and if I shouldn't appear within a reasonable time, forget that we've ever had this conversation. Forget me. Bliss is away from Peking, but when he returns he'll no doubt resume his relationship with you. Don't mention your father to him. If he — or anyone else — should inquire about this conversation with me insist that you thought the whole time you were talking to Bliss. Understand?"

David could only nod.

"Any questions?"

The boy was in a quandary. Bliss had long tried to convince him that it was his "duty" to forget his father, and there was a strong possibility that this was another trap. If he snatched the bait he would be in trouble again with the man who had become his guardian, and the punishment inflicted on him by the turncoat was always harsh.

On the other hand, there was something about the man now looming over him that seemed genuine. He looked like Bliss, of course, and sounded like him too. But there were differences. His eyes weren't precisely the same, and perhaps his voice was a slight shade deeper and more resonant.

It was difficult, almost impossible, for David to believe that the father who, in his opinion, had abandoned him, had suddenly reappeared in the guise of Richard L. Bliss. However, he could imagine no reason why Bliss would resort to such an elaborate scheme just to trick, and subsequently, punish him. Looking back over the past few years, he knew that his guardian needed no excuse at all to reprimand him and exact a penalty from him.

Unable to make up his mind, the boy decided

to play it safe. Still silent, he shook his head.

"I'm trying to think of your safety," Larry persisted. "If there's anything that isn't clear to you, anything you want to know, ask it now."

David remained mute.

"You'll come to the apartment, then, after you're finished marching in the parade?"

It was disturbing to hear such gentleness from Bliss, who had no humility and loved to give orders.

"I — guess so."

Larry knew he had to conceal his own sense of panic at his son's unexpected lack of cooperation. He couldn't blame the boy, of course, for being suspicious and defensive, but he hadn't seriously considered the possibility that David might refuse to participate in an escape attempt. "I'm counting on you," Larry said firmly. "Don't let me down. Or yourself."

David's face was empty of all expression.

Larry, looking past him toward the main building of the academy, saw Headmaster Wong come out of his office and glance in their direction. "When Bliss comes out here to see you, how long does he stay?"

"Just a few minutes."

"Then we'd better start back." Larry hesitated, resisting the strong temptation to put a hand on his son's shoulder. For one thing,

David might shrink from his touch, and for another, Wong might be startled by a gesture so uncharacteristic of Bliss.

Neither spoke again as they walked toward the headmaster, whose professional smile was blandly genial.

David drew himself erect, stood at attention, and gave the Communist salute. "Thank you for your instruction, Comrade Bliss," he said somberly.

"I hope it will be of benefit to you." Larry saw — or imagined that he saw — a hint of suppressed excitement in his son's eyes. Perhaps he had managed to get through to the boy after all. He would know in another forty-eight hours, if everything went well.

"I understand from young Heddon," he said to Wong, "that he will be at liberty for some hours after the students take part in the parade on the day after tomorrow. I've told him to come to my apartment in the city as soon as he is released."

The headmaster frowned. "It was my intention to send him back out here at the end of the parade. He must be penalized for his unprovoked and barbaric assault on the grandson of our beloved Marshal Chen."

"I've forced him to tell me the whole story of that unhappy incident, Comrade Wong, and I shall deal with him in my own way."

The headmaster scowled more deeply. "When the comrade marshal hears of the fight he will demand to know what punitive steps the academy authorities have taken."

Larry could not permit a fussy little man to spoil his one possible chance to save his son. "I'll take full responsibility with Marshal Chen," he said firmly.

Wong's eyes widened, and Larry knew instantly that he had erred. The head of a sub-department in the intelligence service was in no position to defy one of the nation's most powerful military officers. But there had been no choice.

5

THE OLDEST PORTIONS of the Temple of the Lion
had remained standing for two thousand years.
The graceful, soaring building had been built
as a palace for General Pan Ch'ao during the
Han dynasty, and through the centuries it had
been the home of emperors, military leaders,
and great noblemen. The "new" wing had been
added during the K'ang Hsi reign in the early
eighteenth century, and most of the improve-
ments made by the modern rulers of China
were invisible.

Everyone could see the triple rows of electrified barbed-wire fences that surrounded the
temple, of course, and the Red flag flying above
the roof was plainly visible. But the electronic
safety devices that protected the complex of
buildings — now the headquarters of the overseas intelligence service — were too subtle for
an outsider to appreciate. Few who came in and
out of the palace realized that they were being

watched by the captain of the guard on closed-circuit television. Fewer still knew that alarm bells would ring and sirens wail if an intruder tried to climb the stone walls that had been worn smooth by the elements. Multicolored lights flashed and winked on huge panels, and operators seated before these consoles were able to follow everyone in the place from office to office, department to department.

The palace was the nerve center of China's vast espionage operations abroad. In rooms to which only a select few were admitted there were huge maps of the entire world, and on them were pins with colored heads. Red indicated the presence of trusted, full-time agents in virtually every nation, on every continent. Green designated men and women who could give only a portion of their time to work for communism, and yellow was used for the all-important couriers and short-wave radio operators who comprised the service's communications system. Here and there were clusters of black pins too, indicating that some agents were considered unreliable and therefore were given only minor functions to perform, jobs that would not compromise the agency's security.

It had been compromised, however. Larry Heddon had memorized considerable quantities of data about the building and the people who worked there. During his six months of training prior to leaving the United States he had studied surreptitiously taken photographs of men and women he might meet there and had spent hours tracing fragmentary but useful diagrams of the palace itself. His ability to feel at home and carry off his disguise in the Temple of the Lion would, more than anything else, determine the success or failure of his mission.

Larry was calm and relaxed as he approached the palace after returning to Peking from his visit to David's school. He felt a glow of well-being that had been absent since the nightmare of Sue's death and David's kidnapping. His reunion with his son, unsatisfactory though it had been, made him feel capable of dealing with any situation that might arise.

The guards stationed at the main entrance checked Larry's forged credentials, found them acceptable, and waved him past the stainless-steel inner gates. But, his confidence increasing, he paused and asked that Hung Hsui be sent to him. As Larry knew, it was part of the normal routine that any official who had been absent from the city was required to check in with the appropriate authority.

The principal custodian, the man charged with the responsibility for the building's security, quickly appeared from his office only a few feet away. Larry recognized him at once from the secret picture taken by an American agent. Like so many northern Chinese, he was tall, with an athletic build; his face was lined, but his manner was deceptively jolly as he approached with the easy grace of a professional athlete.

"Ah, Comrade Bliss," he said. "You've been away."

"Yes." Larry offered no explanation as they shook hands, and none was expected. In China, as in other countries, executives of an espionage organization did not discuss their travels, even with each other.

"Your voyage appears to have agreed with you, Comrade Bliss. You've regained the weight you lost."

Larry smiled, and was pleased that he had gained a small tidbit of information. Bliss, it appeared, had made a journey out of China by ship.

"One moment." Hung Hsui disappeared into his office, returning a few moments later with a file folder in his hand. "I'll need your signature on the new monthly admission form."

It was difficult to forge another man's signature, but Larry was prepared to do so. He had copied Richard L. Bliss's handwriting in many long, tiring hours of practice, preparing for a contingency of just this sort. Accepting the pen and printed form, he wrote Bliss's name with a flourish, then held his breath for an instant as Hung Hsui compared the signature with that on a previously submitted form.

"You'd think," Larry said lightly, "that the people in the administrative security office had nothing better to do than invent new forms to bedevil all of us."

"They haven't." The custodian sighed and, apparently finding the signature in order, slipped the paper Larry had just signed into the folder.

Here, perhaps, was an opportunity to glean some vitally needed information. If a new set of Bliss's fingerprints was necessary to accompany the new forms, Larry would be in trouble. "It's a wonder they don't ask you to take our fingerprints every time we come in and out. Then you and your staff would be racing all over the building."

"Don't make such jokes aloud, Comrade Bliss. My legs ache when I think of it." Hung Hsui turned away with a weary smile.

Larry's attempt had failed, but he had lost nothing, either. Waving cordially to the principal custodian, he walked straight to the central staircase that emperors had once descended.

Concentrating on the details he had been provided of the building's layout, he walked to the second floor, turned left, and went down a broad corridor to Room 17. Until he learned

76

to associate individuals with the photographs and descriptions he had studied it was safer not to make his way through a large outer office where many staff members worked. So, instead, he opened a door adjacent to number 17 and saw a young woman working at a desk.

"Good morning, Comrade L'ang," he said.

The secretary seemed surprised, but was not alarmed. Larry's disguise was so good that Bliss's secretary, who ordinarily worked closely with him every day, was completely fooled. "A thousand welcomes, Comrade Bliss," she replied.

Larry paused momentarily. "Is there any urgent business that needs my attention before I look through my mail?"

"No, sir. Comrade Williams is handling the Montreal matter. Comrade Butterfield's contact in Washington has been arrested by the Americans, but he's a man who knows very little about us, and Comrade P'eng and the others upstairs aren't too worried."

Larry nodded. He had known that Washington had intended to apprehend a minor Chinese spy in order to distract attention from his own entrance into China. "Tell no one I'm here," he directed. "I want to work undisturbed until I can clear off my desk."

A moment later he was in the inner sanctum of Richard L. Bliss. Closing the door behind him, he silently slid a bolt into place, locking himself in. Then he went to work with feverish but orderly haste. He had only the rest of the afternoon and the following day to find the data that General Hopkins was so anxious to have.

He had been instructed to look through the desk first, and he followed orders. Ignoring the unopened mail stacked neatly in a wicker basket at one side of the large desk, he went through the drawers one by one. He found many trivial papers relating to the activities of Chinese operatives in the United States and Canada, but paid no attention to them. "Unless you run across something really sensational," General Hopkins had told him in a final briefing session, "don't bother with extras. It will be difficult for you to memorize any very considerable amount of information so concentrate on the essentials."

The contents of the desk were interesting, but weren't what Larry was seeking. Neither were the things he found in folders piled on a table behind the desk. All governments thrived on long memos, and that of China was no exception. Twilight came and he snapped on an overhead light, realizing he had another hour, at most, to work tonight. Employees of the agency were expected to leave by seven o'clock in the evening, or if they stayed later, had to get special clearance from the principal custodian. Having already chatted with Hung Hsui, Larry didn't want to call further attention to himself.

Most of the building's employees were already gone for the day; it was very quiet outside the private office; and Larry knew that the time had come for him to devote his full attention to the safe in the far corner. In the cap of the fountain pen was a strong acid that would eat through metal and enable him to open the iron safe if other methods failed, but he had been told to rely on his own skill first, and use the acid only if everything else failed.

First he examined the outside of the strongbox to make certain that no electric or electronic alarm devices were attached to it. He found none, and kneeling in front of the safe, began to spin the dial.

There were new safes these days that were virtually burglar-proof, but Larry had good cause to be thankful that China was a decade or two behind the other advanced nations of the world in its technology. The safe was an old-fashioned kind, and he had been taught the technique of breaking combinations during his training. Everything depended on the sensitivity of his fingers and the acuteness of his hearing.

Not looking at the dial, he held his ear close

79

to it, twisting it very slowly, first to the left and then to the right. The operation required patience, his instructors had told him, and under no circumstances could he allow himself to become flustered.

Opening safes at an intelligence school in Pennsylvania was in no way similar to doing the real thing in Peking, and for some minutes Larry's fingers felt stiff and clumsy. But he gradually forced himself to relax, and after a time began to hear and feel the tiny clicking sounds that indicated that the inner tumblers were falling into their appropriate slots.

There was a louder click as the dial came to a halt on a turn to the right. Larry, his hands clammy and his collar wet with perspiration, raised the handle and opened the door of the safe.

All the documents in the safe were bordered in green and red, meaning they were classified as top secret. Most of them, Larry found as he leafed through them, were records of past operations and had no direct bearing on his present search.

At last, however, he came to a folder marked "San Francisco," and in it discovered a single sheet of paper bearing some cryptic figures and Chinese character symbols. He could almost hear General Hopkins saying to him, "Somewhere in Bliss's office, probably in his safe, you'll find a reference to the vault number of his current operations file. The file itself will most likely be in the vault."

Larry copied the number, replaced everything he had taken from the safe, and closed it. As he was spinning the dial, there was a sudden knock at the door, and he jumped.

"Richie, are you in there?" The voice was that of a woman, who was speaking English with a strong European accent Larry couldn't immediately identify.

"Who is it?"

"Laura, of course." She sounded a trifle annoyed. "I saw your light, so I knew you were back. Please let me in, Richie."

He went to the door reluctantly. Here, in person, was the woman about whom his instructors had told him nothing.

The woman was a blonde in her late thirties, sufficiently attractive to look appealing in her padded tunic and trousers of dull gray. To Larry's embarrassment, she raised her face to his as she closed the door behind her.

He kissed her lightly, a gesture she seemed to expect as her due.

"Well," she said, making no attempt to hide her displeasure. "Did you get my note?"

Larry realized that he now faced a particularly difficult test. It was one thing for him to fool Bliss's casual acquaintances and even the people who worked for him, but quite another matter to fill the other man's shoes in dealing with a woman who looked intelligent and perceptive, and who seemed to be a close friend. "I read it when I stopped off at the apartment this morning," he told her. "But I haven't had a minute to myself all day." That much was the literal truth.

She helped herself to a cigarette from a box on the desk, lit it, and looked him up and down slowly. "You're the most incredible man I've ever known."

"Am I?" Larry countered.

"Anyone else in your spot," Laura said, pronouncing the word as *zpot*, "would have turned into a skeleton in this past month. But you've put on ten pounds."

Bliss, he gathered, was in real difficulties of some sort.

"You must have nerves of steel, Richie."

Playing for time and more information, Larry shrugged.

"I didn't think you'd actually get my note." She paced up and down, her incongruously high-heeled shoes clicking on the tile floor. "I sent it on the off chance that you'd actually be foolish enough to come back here."

"What did you think I'd do?" he asked, trying to draw her out.

"Stay in Singapore, naturally!" Laura's

voice rose and became shrill. Trying to calm herself, she went to the window that looked down on the main entrance to the temple, and stood there, smoking furiously. "The Russian consul there would have provided you with a private plane to Moscow, and you'd have been greeted with open arms in the Kremlin."

Bliss, Larry thought, must truly be in a desperate situation if, as it appeared, he had contemplated defecting to the Russians.

"I have a right to know the truth," Laura said. "Why did you come back?"

"A man in this business is respected by no one if he betrays his employers." Larry had to temporize, in order to learn more.

She looked at him contemptuously. "But you did, Richie! Even now, after all that's happened in the past six months, you still believe the Chinese trust you. How naïve you are! Did you think Comrade P'eng was joking when he threatened to have your head at the last meeting of the executive board?"

Larry realized he had to play the role of Bliss to the hilt. "I still believe in justice, Laura, which is why I became a Communist."

"Then you should have stayed in America," she replied with brutal irony. "As for me, I'm going to Warsaw when my contract expires in April. I've had enough of these Chinese. They hate all foreigners, no matter what our nationality. It's the Boxer Rebellion attitude all over again."

Larry now knew that Laura was Polish, but the revelation had little significance. Too many other things were on his mind.

"For me, enough is more than enough. And you're an imbecile, Richie."

"I prefer to take my chances here."

"Oh, I'm not really blaming you. I have my passport, after all, and there's at least a surface friendship between the Polish presidium and these people. But you're completely at the mercy of the Chinese." She restlessly moved away from the window. "Forgive me for scolding you, my dear. This country is depressing after a time. I've just received a box of food — real food — from Warsaw. So come to my apartment with me this evening, and let me cook you dinner."

Larry glanced at his watch and saw that only a little more than a half hour remained before the seven-o'clock curfew. Perhaps, he thought, he could utilize the help of this woman without tipping his hand to her. It was worth the try, and might save valuable time. "I wish I could accept," he said, "but I'm not finished here."

"More of your excuses?"

"I mean it. I've got to check some finger-prints in personnel, and there's a paper I want to read in the vaults."

"That shouldn't take long."

"I hope not," he said, and meant it. Now was the moment to suggest that she guide him through the building he knew only from the sketches he had studied. "Come along, if you like, and then we can do something about dinner."

Laura seemed pleased. "I'll get my coat and meet you in the corridor." She left, her high heels tapping on the floors.

Larry made certain that everything was in order and turned off the lights. A few moments later the woman joined him in the outer hall.

"Why must you check fingerprints yourself? That lazy girl who works for you has done nothing for weeks but trim her nails."

Larry made no reply and let her take the lead as they walked to the central staircase and climbed to the next higher floor. In spite of all he had learned about this place, there were gaps in his knowledge. American intelligence was far from perfect. He knew only that the fingerprint cards and other personal data on all employees of the bureau were located in a maze of offices on the third floor, and he was thankful for the unwitting services of this chattering woman.

"Why on earth should you have to look at some prints anyway, Richie? You haven't gone back into operations work yourself, have you?"

It was easy, under the circumstances, for

Larry to react as Bliss himself might have done. "Laura," he snapped, "you ask too many questions."

She was visibly miffed, and did not speak again.

They came to an office in which an elderly Chinese was sitting at a small desk. Behind him were long rows of wooden filing cabinets, and Larry had to force himself to remain calm. It was imperative that he find and destroy Richard L. Bliss's fingerprint records, the only positive method of identification that could prove the man impersonating Bliss an impostor.

The old man stood and bowed. "Can I be of service to you, Comrade Bliss?"

"There's a personnel file I want to check."

"May I get it for you?"

"I prefer to get it myself." Larry knew he had to invent a valid-sounding reason. "Comrade P'eng," he said, using the name of the supervisor of intelligence operations, "has asked for a confidential report on someone."

The man accepted the explanation without question, and waved Larry toward the files.

Laura, however, looked surprised, and Larry understood why. If P'eng was out to ruin Bliss, as she had told him just a little while ago, the last person in the entire headquarters P'eng would use as a confidant would be Richard L. Bliss.

Larry was afraid he had made a serious mistake, but couldn't retract what he had said and had to proceed accordingly. He walked quickly down the aisle, noting the alphabetical listings, and then turned a corner into another aisle with wooden cabinets on both sides. It was difficult to act as though he was familiar with a filing system he had never before seen, but each case was labeled, and he soon oriented himself.

Outwardly crisp and efficient, he finally found a section marked "Employees of Foreign Birth," and, opening the right drawer, drew out a Manila envelope containing the records of Richard L. Bliss. A hasty search revealed the card containing ten neatly inked fingerprints, and he felt a wave of relief.

But there were footsteps at the end of the aisle behind him. Glancing over his shoulder, he saw Laura, who, making no attempt to conceal her curiosity, was sauntering toward him.

Larry had been taught what to do in an emergency like this. He stuffed the card into his mouth and, as he painfully chewed and swallowed it, replaced the envelope and picked up another.

His mouth and throat were raw, but by the time Laura reached his side he had just swallowed the last of the card. Now, with the vital data destroyed, no one in China could prove that he was anyone other than Richard L. Bliss.

Laura smiled disarmingly as she edged still closer.

Larry turned away from her so that his shoulder blocked her view of the meaningless envelope he had snatched from the file. Then, after pretending for a moment or two that he was still examining the papers in it, he replaced them and deliberately let her see that he was replacing the envelope in the drawer under the letter "G."

Should she be questioned by investigators at some future time, she might remember that he had drawn a card for a name beginning with a letter other than his own. But he was relying on a slim reed. If and when the authorities found Bliss's fingerprint card missing, Laura would be in a position to tell them that the supposed turncoat had spent time examining the files of employees of foreign birth. Even though no one would be able to prove that he had removed the record of Bliss's fingerprints, the circumstantial evidence against him would be strong.

"That's that," he said, and closed the drawer.

Laura continued to smile. "I'd like very much to know what you're doing."

"It will be much healthier for you to mind

your own business." They started together up the aisle toward the old man's desk.

"I'm willing to bet a case of good Polish vodka that Comrade P'eng gave you no assignment here."

Larry didn't want to be drawn into a discussion of this touchy point. He thanked the elderly custodian of the personnel files, exchanged bows with the man, and hurried out into the corridor.

Laura was close behind him. "Tell me what this is all about, Richie."

"I've got to be in and out of the vaults in seventeen minutes." He knew from the sketches he had studied that the top-secret documents were kept in the cellar of the building, and he half walked, half ran down the stairs, the woman keeping up with him as best she could.

"Why all the secrecy?" she persisted. "Especially with me!"

It wasn't difficult for Larry to simulate impatient anger. "Please, Laura! Not now, and not here, of all places!" Later, he knew, he would have to dream up a cover story that sounded logical enough to satisfy her and keep her at least temporarily quiet.

But right now the most ticklish and dangerous part of his mission loomed directly ahead, and he had to concentrate on it, remembering every infinitesimal detail of his instructions.

"Why don't you wait for me at the entrance?" he suggested as they reached the ground floor and started toward the stairs that led to the underground chambers.

"I assure you I have no intention of going into that chamber of horrors, my dear. Even if I had permission to use the vaults, I'd have nightmares for a month if I went near the place." She opened her handbag, lit a cigarette, and gave him a mock salute. "Don't forget to come out, Richie. I've heard that people have disappeared down there and have never been seen again."

Larry returned her wave and promptly dismissed her from his mind. Uniformed guards armed with submachine guns were stationed outside a pair of thick metal doors similar to those at the entrance to safety-deposit vaults in American banks. When Larry reached the bottom of the stairs, both covered him with their weapons, and one pushed a buzzer on the wall beside him.

A key turned in the lock of a steel door, and a young officer, automatic pistol in his right hand, came into the dimly lighted entrance hall.

"Your name, department, and business, comrade," he said.

"Richard L. Bliss, department forty-two, with a request to see certain documents."

"Do you have the file number?"

"Right here."

The officer inspected the sheet of paper on which Larry had scribbled the figures and Chinese character symbols. "Are you carrying firearms?"

Larry hesitated for only a fraction of a second. If he denied that he had a gun and was searched, he would be in immediate, serious trouble. "Here," he said, and surrendered his automatic.

The officer examined it, looking with special interest at the silencer attachment, and then waved Larry through the door.

They went into a somewhat larger steel-lined chamber, at the far end of which stood another pair of heavy bank vault doors at least eight inches thick. A hard-faced lieutenant colonel was sitting at a small desk, a pistol in a holster strapped around his waist, and he went through the same formula. "Your name, department, and business?"

Larry repeated what he had said a moment earlier.

The lieutenant colonel motioned him to a chair and gave him a brief form to fill out.

Larry made the necessary notations on it, then signed Bliss's name.

The officer went to a card index file and compared the signature with that on a card. Then he returned to his desk and, picking up his telephone, dialed a number. He conversed briefly, speaking so softly that Larry couldn't hear what he said. Replacing the instrument in its cradle, he nodded.

Larry glanced at his watch and saw that only eight minutes remained now before seven o'clock, when he would need special permission to stay in the building.

The lieutenant colonel called to someone in a guardroom off to his left, and a captain appeared, two armed guards behind him. "Take Comrade Bliss into the vaults." He pulled an electrically operated level, and one of the huge doors swung open on silent hinges.

The captain, holding the form that Larry had made out, and the guards ranged themselves on either side of the visitor. The outer door closed silently, and Larry was alone with the three sentries.

Feeble lights burned overhead, shining dimly on long rows of reinforced steel cabinets. The floor was of heavy metal too, and so was the ceiling. The men who had designed this vault had left nothing to chance, and only a direct hit by a high-powered bomb would destroy it.

They halted at last before a cabinet at least a hundred and fifty feet from the entrance, and the captain inserted a key into the lock of a cabinet. "Your key, Comrade Bliss," he demanded, and held out his hand.

Larry was dismayed. Apparently the system here was similar to that used by the owners of safety-deposit boxes in the United States. The custodians had one key, and the depositor kept another. A box would open only when both were inserted in the appropriate locks.

No one had prepared him for this contingency, and he had no key.

The data he had come so far to obtain was only a few feet away, but he was afraid that, for all practical purposes, he might as well be back in Pennsylvania.

All he could do was go through the motions of reaching confidently into the pocket in which he kept Bliss's wallet. He brought it out, and then looked up in surprise. At least his chagrin was real.

First he cursed softly in Cantonese, the most colorful of Chinese dialects, and then said, "I'm sorry, Comrade Captain, but my key is locked in the principal safe of my department."

The captain looked at his own watch and grimaced. "In six minutes I'm off duty. If I wait while you send for it, we'll be here for at least another hour."

Larry saw a faint ray of hope. "If we could get the master key, we could still be out of here on time."

The captain was exasperated. "You administrative people are all alike. You'd lose your feet if they weren't attached to your legs. I have a dinner engagement, and I don't intend to be late for it. Chung, get the master key from the colonel. And hurry."

One of the sentries hurried off.

"You realize, Comrade Bliss, that it will be necessary to make an official report of your carelessness, and that it will go on your permanent record."

"Of course." Larry hid his wild elation and shrugged.

The sentry returned with another key, a metal box was removed from the steel cabinet, and the captain carried it to a plain table of unvarnished wood that was completely bare, lacking writing materials of any kind. He snapped on a light overhead and waved Larry to the box.

His hands trembling, Larry sat down, while the captain stood nearby, too far to see what was written on the papers that were taken from the box, yet close enough to make certain that none were removed permanently.

Larry quickly found the file marked "San Francisco," and began reading it. There was far too much material for him to absorb in a short time, so he concentrated on the essentials — an address in San Francisco's Chinatown and the names of four people who appeared more prominently than any others in the text.

"It's three minutes before seven, comrade," the captain said.

Memorization was perhaps the most important of all phases of intelligence work for an agent in the field, and Larry had spent at least two hours each day during his six months of training learning to commit facts to memory at little more than a glance. He tried to imprint the San Francisco address and the names on his mind, but an unexpected sense of panic numbed him.

In sheer desperation he calmed himself, knowing that it was unlikely that he would get another chance to examine the papers.

For better or worse he did his best, put the papers back into the box, and stood. "I'm ready, comrade," he said.

The captain put the box back into its niche, locked the cabinet, and trotted back toward the entrance.

Larry, at his heels, felt weak, and his hands were clammy. He repeated the names and address to himself silently, praying he could not forget them. There were so many details in the documents that Washington would have found useful, but it served no purpose to wish that he'd had more time to study the papers.

He was passed out through the intricate security doors, his gun was returned to him, and he reached the ground floor with only ninety seconds to spare. A few others were rushing out of the building, and Laura, who was standing just inside the entrance, was puffing nervously on another cigarette.

Only now, as Larry joined her and they went out into the raw Peking night, did Larry fully realize and appreciate what he had done. Provided he could remember the address and names — and was not revealed as an imposter — he had accomplished the major part of the assignment that General Hopkins had given him.

But this was no time to congratulate himself or to celebrate. He was still in China, an uncooperative David might cause complications, and escape was a yet-to-be-accomplished dream.

6

LAURA'S SMALL APARTMENT was furnished in
European style with comfortable if slightly
old-fashioned furniture. She proved herself
a charming hostess and an excellent cook, giving Larry a dinner of borsht, beef with a gar-
nish of sour cream, mushrooms, and mild pep-
pers, and a honey cake from a recipe that dated
back to the eleventh century.

In spite of the unexpectedly pleasant inter-
lude, however, Larry felt as though he was
walking on eggs all evening. At first they discussed such impersonal subjects as the reper-
tory of the Peking opera company and the Chinese pantomime plays that were currently the
rage in Shanghai, both topics on which Larry's
intelligence tutors had briefed him thoroughly.

But her insistence that he drink some of her
Polish vodka became increasingly embarrassing, and she was watching him far too closely
for comfort.

"Richie," Laura said at last as they finished their third cups of black chicory-flavored coffee, "you don't seem yourself at all."

Larry smiled with feigned indolence. "What makes you think that?"

"I've never known you to refuse a drink, and you've always been wild about this brand of vodka."

"I could claim that I'm a changed man," he replied, choosing his words with care. "But the truth of the matter is that I prefer to be completely sober. You yourself indicated that I'm in a somewhat dangerous spot, and I want to have my wits about me."

His explanation seemed to make sense to her, and she nodded as, curled up on the sofa in her living room, she fitted a cigarette into a long holder. "There's a great deal about your situation that I don't know."

"I won't deny it," Larry said.

"I've been waiting to hear everything."

He shifted in his chair and looked out through the frosted windowpane.

"I've been worried sick ever since P'eng denounced you. Did you know that your automobile was permanently returned to the state pool three or four weeks ago?"

"I'm not surprised." Larry was privately disappointed. Bliss's automobile would have been useful in an attempted escape from Peking.

"And the rumors I've heard!"

"For instance?"

"When I was having lunch the other day at the commune several people seemed certain that you'd never come back from Singapore."

"I'm here." Larry paused for an instant. "What made them think I wouldn't show up again?"

Laura unconsciously lowered her voice. "I can't prove this, of course. No one can. But I believe that Ho F'ang himself may be investigating you."

"I see." Larry saw a great deal. Many hours of his training had been devoted to a study in depth of the operations of Ho F'ang Tio Wang, the head of the nation's dreaded counterintelligence organization, the Security Service. If Bliss was in trouble with Ho F'ang, then Larry, impersonating Bliss, was in even greater difficulties than he had imagined.

"I don't want to frighten you unnecessarily, Richie."

"I appreciate the favor."

"You can return it," Laura said, "by bringing me up to date on what you're doing, including those visits to other offices just before the curfew tonight."

Larry knew he had to face the problem as directly as possible, and he wanted, too, to help an innocent woman avoid becoming implicated in his own situation. "If Ho F'ang is

99

investigating me," he said, "the less you know, the better it will be for you, Laura. I'm thinking of your best interests."

"What unusual nobility." There was gentle irony in her tone.

"I mean it. Forget today, forget all you've heard, and forget everything that has ever happened in the past."

"As if I could!"

"Ho F'ang has been known to use rough methods at times."

"He wouldn't dare, with me. I still carry my Polish passport."

"I hope for your sake that you're right. He isn't noted for respecting subjects of even the friendliest countries."

Laura looked at him for a long time. "I'm not sure whether you're really being kind, Richie, or whether you're hiding something from me."

"Give me the benefit of the doubt."

"I'll try. But you're really different, you know. I'm trying to figure out just what it is about you that's not the same."

Larry knew the time had come to beat a cautious retreat. He would be taking too great a risk if he allowed himself to be subjected to a detailed character analysis. He stood. "Let's save your opinions for some other time, Laura, if you don't mind. I've had a long trip," he added truthfully. "And I'm exhausted."

She rose too and walked with him to the front hall, where he had left his hat and coat. "Will I see you at the office tomorrow?"

"I think not."

"More mysterious activities?"

Larry merely smiled.

The woman raised her face for another kiss, and Larry thanked her with genuine warmth for a pleasant evening. Then he started out through the now-deserted streets for Bliss's apartment.

So far, thanks to a combination of skill, obedience to orders, and good luck, he was unscathed. He had collected less information than he had wanted to take back to Washington, but had nevertheless acquired more than enough to justify the time and effort that had been spent by the United States on his mission. If he succeeded in getting out of China alive his venture would be considered highly successful.

Once again he remembered the instructions and admonitions of General Hopkins: "You'll be strictly on your own, Larry. You'll have to make your own arrangements to smuggle you and your son out of China. There's one man who can help you, but don't go to him. He'll be keeping watch over you for us, and you can depend on him to do what he can for you if you get into serious difficulties. I can't give you his name or tell you where to find him, be-

cause he's our most important permanent
agent in China and we can't risk losing him
or the people who work with him. If you must,
go to Mao Square — the place where the statue
of the dowager empress once stood — and
walk around the pool where they kept carp
during the summers in the old days. But don't
go there unless your situation is desperate."

Larry grinned wearily. He had no need for
the help of America's secret agents in China.
At the moment he was too tired to think clearly, but after a good sleep he would have a day
and night to plan the escape route he and
David would take — assuming, of course, that
he could persuade the boy to go with him.

His superiors in Washington had spent
hours debating the problem of his departure
from China and had finally decided that he
would have to improvise as best he could.
"We'll keep a submarine off the coast for you,"
General Hopkins had said. "And if you've got
to use our agents they'll try to make contact
with the ship for you. But don't count on it,
either for your own escape or any other purpose. At best it would be a long-shot chance
just trying to make the contact. And so many
things can happen once you're inside the country that you'll be better off if you make your
own plans. That's one reason we're sending
you rather than someone else. This job needs
a man who really knows China."

Larry reached the apartment building and yawned as he climbed the stairs to Bliss's apartment. For the present it was enough to repeat once again the names and address of the Chinese agents in San Francisco. Tomorrow he would work out his next step.

He unlocked the door, switched on the light, and stiffened. Three uniformed men armed with submachine guns had been sitting in the dark room waiting for him.

Larry reached for his automatic, but it was too late. Two of the men grasped his arms while the third covered him with a gun.

"Comrade Bliss," the leader of the group said, "you will come with us."

More than half a million men, women, and children marched beneath the huge arches of the Ch'ien Men Gate, chanting slogans and singing the songs of the Chinese revolution. More than a million others lined the old Imperial Road to cheer them, and although the day was bitterly cold, excitement ran high.

Vendors wheeling little carts on which portable charcoal braziers were mounted did a brisk business in roasted watermelon seeds. Others, selling rice cakes, were often surrounded by eager throngs, and the sellers of scalding tea soon ran out of their supply. Countless thousands swarmed around the Great Hall of the People, the largest auditorium in Peking, to watch the leaders of the government, the military services, the Communist party and other high-ranking dignitaries descend from their luxurious cars — American, German, and Russian limousines — to attend a long session of speech making.

The boys from the Sun Yat-sen Academy for Boys, who had marched past the reviewing stand before noon, were part of the huge crowd outside the hall. They applauded vigorously as each of China's leaders appeared and went into the building. David Heddon clapped his hands with the rest, automatically, but actually paid little attention to the proceedings. Every few minutes he looked at his wristwatch, and at one o'clock he knew that the time had come for him to leave.

He caught the eye of the headmaster, who actually seemed relieved to see him go, and then slipped away from his classmates. The holiday crowds were thick, and a feeling of unreality gripped David as he made his way slowly through them. He felt a rare sense of excitement, too. He wasn't sure why he was obeying the request of the man who had looked like his guardian, and he still suspected that Bliss was intending, for some unknown reason, to trap and punish him. But there was an outside chance that the man might actually be his father. In any event, he had little to lose. Bliss had treated him so harshly in the past that even a summer at a corrective labor camp didn't mean much any more.

Not that he felt any great love for his father. After all, a father who really loved his son could have done something to get him out of China in all these years. But maybe there was more to his story than David knew. One thing was certain. The fantasies that Bliss had spun for him were transparent lies, and he'd like to hear his father's version of what had happened.

The bamboo blinds were tightly closed on every floor of the apartment house, and David hesitated for an instant as he approached the building. Then, annoyed with himself, he went into the entrance hall. He had made up his mind to learn more about the strange matter, and this was no time to let his fears get the better of him.

He closed the outer door behind him, and as he started toward the staircase the door of the ground-floor apartment opened and the landlady stood in the frame.

"What do you want, boy?"

"I'm Comrade Bliss's ward. He asked me to meet him here this afternoon."

"He isn't here."

"But —"

"I tell you, he isn't here!"

The boy held his ground. "When will he return?"

"I have no idea. Now go away!" The woman's ferocity was startling.

David saw that she was upset, but before he could question her again, she slammed her door. He walked out into the street, feeling curiously let down, not knowing what to do next.

After casting about for a solution to his problem, hesitating and faltering, he finally reached a decision. He'd been told to come to the apartment, but had been disappointed. So there was only one other place he could go: Bliss's office. After all, he'd been there before, on the few occasions when Bliss had sent for him. In fact Bliss had made quite a point of telling him that his name was on the approved visitors' list — as though it were an honor.

David knew there was a risk involved. If the man was Bliss, he might become angry at being interrupted. If it was his father, on the other hand, he might have a thousand reasons for not wanting to see David there. But the boy couldn't go back to the academy — and wait in a vacuum of ignorance. It was better to know something, if possible, and to take the chance that Bliss would reprimand him.

He threaded his way through the large crowds in the Forbidden City, and it was almost two o'clock when he approached the Temple of the Lion. There the crowds thinned abruptly. The residents of Peking, like other

Chinese, had learned not to be too curious, and the approach to the ancient palace was deserted.

David climbed the broad steps of stone that had been worn smooth through the centuries and stopped at the entrance, where several rifle-bearing guards scowled at him. He gave them his name, told them he had come to see Comrade Richard L. Bliss, and was ordered to wait.

After a brief delay an officer came out of an office, compared David with a photograph, and ordered him to sign his name on several forms. Then a guard was assigned to guide him to the second-floor office.

"I know the way," David said, but the man paid no attention.

When they reached Room 17 David went at once to the private door beside the main entrance, and the guard nodded, then waited outside. The secretary wasn't at her desk, so David walked straight to the inner door and tapped. There was no reply. He tapped again and finally, taking a deep breath, turned the knob. Bliss's private office was empty too.

The boy went inside, closing the door behind him. Perhaps his father — or Bliss — was busy elsewhere, and would join him shortly. He sat down in a chair opposite the desk.

Moments later, a blond woman came into the office. "Ah, I saw you as I was about to enter my own office down the hall. You are Richie's American ward?"

"Yes, ma'am," David said.

"Permit me to introduce myself. I am Laura Zandulsky."

David clicked his heels and bowed slightly from the waist.

"What are you doing here?" Laura inquired.

"Comrade Bliss asked me to meet him at his apartment this afternoon, but he wasn't there. I thought I might find him here."

Laura frowned. "Why did Comrade Bliss send for you?"

"It concerned — an incident at the academy," David answered warily.

She dismissed schoolboy matters with a shrug and suddenly addressed the boy in English. "He told you nothing of his personal affairs?"

"No, ma'am. Comrade Bliss has never discussed such things with me." David spoke in English too, and was now fully on his guard.

Laura stared at him for a moment, her pale blue eyes troubled. "I don't think he'll be keeping an appointment with you — or anyone else — today."

"I — I hope he isn't ill."

"I hope not." She started to turn away, then changed her mind. "Have you ever heard of a man named Ho F'ang Tio Wang?"

David nodded. Ho F'ang-sen, the man's nephew, was enrolled in one of the lower classes at the academy, and although it was customary for the younger boys to take orders from the older, everyone — including faculty members and even the headmaster himself — treated Ho F'ang-sen with great respect. It was rumored that he was related to a man so powerful that even the members of the ruling presidium were in awe of him. But David had never learned any details. Like the other boys, he avoided the nephew.

"It may be," Laura said unhappily, "that Richie has been taken somewhere by Ho F'ang Tio Wang."

David saw tears in her eyes as she turned quickly and left the room.

The puzzled boy tried to analyze the situation. If Bliss was in difficulty, he wasn't in the least disturbed. But suppose that the man who had come to him at the academy had really been his father — and the authorities had penetrated his masquerade? A sense of alarm shot through David.

There was nothing he could do here, he thought, and went out into the corridor, where the sentry was waiting for him. As they reached the lobby, several men looked in the boy's direction, talking rapidly.

Then two burly soldiers in the brown tunics

and trousers of the Security Service came toward him, each with an automatic in a holster slung from a belt.

"You are the boy called Heddon?" one of them asked in the Hopeh dialect.

"Yes, comrade." David hoped he didn't look as frightened as he suddenly felt.

The man grinned at his companion. "Ho F'ang will be pleased that we located him so easily."

David found himself between them, being led from the building to a waiting automobile, a Russian Volga. There were two other men in the front seat, both of them hard-faced.

No one spoke. David was seated between the pair in the rear seat, and the car started off. It gathered speed quickly, and David jumped when a siren began to scream. Pedestrians scattered as the car raced through the streets of Peking.

7

A ROARING FIRE BLAZED in the hearth of the bedroom in the villa east of Peking. The view from the windows of the snug room was spectacular: rolling, rugged hills, most of them snow-covered, stretched toward the horizons on the north and south. Directly to the east no more than one hundred yards away loomed the vast bulk of the Great Wall, even more impressive at this distance than it was from afar. Massive stones had been fitted together with such skill and cunning that no mortar had been necessary to keep the wall intact. It had been standing for thousands of years, Peking's guardian since the pre-Christian era, and neither time nor man had destroyed this monument to the early emperors of China.

The grounds of the villa were surrounded by a high fence of steel mesh, which was electrified and, as a further safety precaution, had two rolls of ugly barbed wire resting on its top.

Guards were stationed on watchtowers fifty feet apart, each armed with a submachine gun, and other guards, also armed and accompanied by vicious, leashed chow dogs, walked sentry beats just inside the fence.

The villa was a headquarters prison maintained by the Security Service for its special captives, and Ho F'ang had made certain that none of his "guests" could escape. Powerful floodlights illuminated the grounds at night, a fleet of high-powered automobiles was kept ready for instant use in the garage, and a helicopter was poised on the roof of the main building. Even if a prisoner managed — through some miracle — to escape from the compound he wouldn't go far before he was caught and returned.

Larry turned to the fire and rubbed his hands. So far he had held his own with Ho F'ang and a team of questioners who had pounded at him for the better part of twenty-four hours, but he didn't know how much longer his good luck would hold. Ho F'ang and his subordinates had revealed only a few facts since the interrogation had started, and Larry had been forced to put together the pieces of a puzzle.

All he had learned was that Richard L. Bliss had left the Chinese mainland by ship on a secret mission, and that men in the employ of Ho F'ang had been under orders to kill him in Singapore. Hence his seeming return to Peking had stunned the officials of the Security Service.

The curious fact was that Ho F'ang had planned to have Bliss murdered on foreign soil rather than simply taking him into custody and executing him. Reading between the lines of the questions directed at him, Larry guessed that some of Bliss's own superiors had remained friendly to him, even though he had incurred the enmity of the man directly above him, Comrade P'eng.

Government departments that were required to work together had to observe amenities if they hoped to maintain harmonious relations. So Ho F'ang had found it necessary to treat Bliss with a measure of respect. That was why Larry had been given this luxurious room in a Security Service villa and had been served excellent meals.

They hadn't been gentle with him, to be sure, but as yet he had not been subjected to any violent physical mistreatment. He had been made to stand for hour after hour, looking into a battery of huge searchlights that had blinded him, while interrogators he hadn't been able to see questioned him ceaselessly. They had pounded at the same points again and again: "When did you come back to Peking from Singapore?" "Did you travel by military or commercial plane?" "Did you meet any foreign representatives while you were out of China? Did you pass along any Chinese state secrets to them?"

Larry had denied the charges against Bliss until he had been hoarse, so bone-weary he had been ready to drop. He had firmly refused to answer other questions, no matter how often they had been asked. But he didn't know how much longer he could hold out.

The bed on the far side of the room was inviting, but every time he went to it the door opened and a guard came in to prevent him from lying down. Obviously he was being watched through a peephole somewhere in the wall, and it was equally plain that the Security Service men intended to wear him down until he told them everything they wanted to know.

So, like it or not, he had to be concerned with Bliss's problems. He believed from what Laura had so strongly hinted to him that Bliss had sold or given information to the Russians. Precisely what information? He would probably never know.

Ironically, by destroying Bliss's fingerprint record, he had stepped all the way into the turncoat's shoes. His captors couldn't prove, now or ever, that he was anyone other than Bliss. But even if their treatment became rougher, he wouldn't be able to tell them what he literally didn't know.

He realized that the Security Service men

suspected he wasn't Bliss, although he hadn't learned why. They were hammering at him on that subject too, trying to establish whether or not he was, in truth, Richard L. Bliss.

Now as never before Larry was grateful for the intelligence briefing he had been given during his months of training. He had been told almost innumerable facts, major and minor, about Bliss's life, habits, ideas, and personal peculiarities. They had been drilled into him so thoroughly that he was able to respond without thinking when the Security Service men tried to trip him. In a sense, he had almost become Bliss.

But the strain was so great that he was afraid he would forget the San Francisco address and names he had memorized. Only by repeating them to himself when he was alone was he able to feel temporarily reassured.

The one bright hope in this nightmare was that his captors hadn't been able to gain enough evidence to imprison or hang the man they thought was Richard L. Bliss. Their continuing interrogations proved that they were still groping. If he had the stamina and will, they might release him.

A tap sounded at the door, and two guards in the now-familiar brown uniforms came into the room. Larry thought his ordeal was about to begin again. But the men surprised him.

"Comrade Ho F'ang asks you to join him," one of them said.

Ho F'ang was waiting in a small ground-floor room paneled with rare inlaid woods and mosaics depicting some of the heroic exploits, real and imagined, of Mao Tse-tung during his years as a Communist outlaw. A tall, fleshy man with a powerful frame, eyes with deceptively sleepy lids, and a thin mouth, Ho F'ang looked more like a doctor or lawyer than a counterespionage executive.

He motioned his prisoner to a chair. "You look tired, Comrade Bliss."

Larry refused to give him the satisfaction of rising to the bait, and shrugged.

Ho F'ang offered him a cigarette.

"I rarely smoke."

"Some food, perhaps?"

"No, thank you. The meals have been satisfactory."

"I'll happily release you as soon as you tell us what we seek from you."

Larry felt a little more sure of himself. "Overseas espionage always cooperates with a sister service — when possible."

"Perhaps our views of what is cooperation and what is not aren't the same."

"You deal with confidential matters, and so do we. All I know, Comrade Ho F'ang, is that my office doesn't run itself. There are matters vital to the welfare of China piling up there."

"Then be frank with me. Why did you go to the personnel card index room in the Temple of the Lion two days ago?"

"Unfortunately," Larry said, "the business of my department is confidential, as I've been telling your men for the past day and night."

Ho F'ang looked annoyed. "I find it highly irregular that the fingerprint records of Comrade Richard Bliss are missing."

Larry laughed. "Why would I remove my own prints?"

"I can imagine no reason — if they're really yours. But if you're an impostor you'd have every reason to want them destroyed."

"I don't know why you should think I'm someone else, but surely I've established my identity to the satisfaction of even the most zealous Security Service agent!"

"You have." Ho F'ang frowned. "Yet you can't be Bliss."

"This is ridiculous!" Larry feigned indignation.

"I agree."

"Then be good enough to release me immediately. I hope you realize I plan to make a full report on this outrage to Comrade P'eng. He becomes disturbed when members of his department are mistreated, and I feel certain he'll take the entire case to the presidium."

"I've already notified Comrade P'eng that we're holding you for temporary questioning."

The key word was "temporary," and Larry, greatly relieved, felt bolder. "I insist that you send me back to Peking at once!"

The heavy-set Chinese official favored his captive with a humorless smile. "You'd be cautious too if our positions were reversed."

Larry decided that his best defense would be a continuation of his attack. "Nothing would make me happier than if they were."

Ho F'ang laughed, and his amusement now was genuine. Then he sobered quickly. "China has many foes," he said, echoing an approach frequently taken by Premier Chou En-lai. "If she is made safe it matters little what becomes of people like you and me."

"It matters to me," Larry retorted, "and it must to you too."

The Security Service chief picked up a paper from a table near his elbow. "Read this and tell me what you think of it."

Larry read the brief document with care. It was signed by a man named Hsiang, apparently one of Ho F'ang's subordinates, and was brutal in its bluntness. Richard L. Bliss, Hsiang reported, had been killed by two of his most reliable men on the Singapore waterfront. No one had witnessed the murder, all identification had been removed from the body, and the Singapore police, completely baffled by the crime, had given it no publicity. "An enemy of the Chinese people," Hsiang concluded, "has been liquidated."

"I must confess," Larry said, "that this gives me a thoroughly uncomfortable feeling."

"Is that your only reaction, Comrade Bliss?"

"No, Comrade Ho F'ang. If you'll forgive me for quoting an American — in this instance, the humorist Mark Twain — the report of my death has been grossly exaggerated. It must be as obvious to you as it is to me that Hsiang is a liar."

"So it would appear," Ho F'ang replied with a sigh. "Frankly, I am confused. For many years Hsiang has been my most trusted agent, and I've never known him to tell an untruth."

Larry spread his hands. "I can only say that I'm right here."

"In our work, as you know, things are often other than what they seem."

It was unnecessary for Larry to simulate annoyance. "I assure you that this isn't the end of the matter. I'm not totally lacking in influence."

"I'm aware of the complications," the Security Service head replied. "Within two or three days I hope to have the question settled. Hsiang has gone off on a holiday, a hunting trip in the hills of Cambodia. Communications there are rather primitive, but I've sent a messenger for him, and if all goes well he'll fly home before the end of the week."

Larry bridled, as he felt certain Bliss would have done. "This is outrageous! Surely you aren't planning to hold me here against my will for several more days!"

"What choice do I have?"

"I insist you release me immediately! Bumbling idiots have already done too much damage to the operations of my department!"

"I hope that within a very short time I can determine beyond doubt whether you're really Comrade Bliss."

Larry didn't like the sound of the comment, and redoubled the fury of his assault. "I haven't yet been told why I'm being held here as a prisoner," he said icily, "much less why your hirelings were instructed to assassinate me. I demand a full explanation."

"You and I have never liked each other, Bliss. You're still too American for my taste, too arrogant and sure of yourself. I'm willing to grant you — here in the privacy of this room, with no witnesses to overhear us — that this matter places me in a very embarrassing situation. The members of the presidium will discount the testimony of my agents — "

The soft ring of a telephone cut short Ho F'ang's reply, and he looked annoyed as he picked up the instrument at his side. "Yes?" he demanded roughly, then softened. "Ah, you've taken him into custody? Excellent. Bring him to me immediately. No, here. I'm

120

not returning to the city until later tonight."
He seemed highly pleased, but suddenly his
mood darkened again. "Well, keep looking
for her. But be careful. The Poles could cause
trouble for us unless we handle this delicately."
The telephone crashed into its cradle.

Larry guessed that Ho F'ang was talking
about Laura and was certain that the real
Bliss would not have sat back meekly, so he
became purposely scornful. "Ho F'ang," he
said, "you are descended from a donkey if you
think I've been conspiring with the Polish
woman who works in my office."

"Comrade P'eng," Ho F'ang said, "is con-
vinced that you're both in the pay of Moscow."

"P'eng," Larry said deliberately, "is also
the great-grandson of a donkey."

"Perhaps. It will be helpful if the woman
decides to cooperate with us. If not, there are
other ways of finding out what I want to
know." Ho F'ang stood, indicating that the interview had come to an end. "Understand one
thing, Comrade Bliss. I must either prove you
guilty or an impostor. My department and I
are too deeply involved in this affair for me
to set you free and give you the chance to complain to the presidium about me." Ho F'ang
pressed a buzzer, the guards appeared, and
Larry was conducted back to the bedroom on
the second floor.

There, when the door was closed and locked behind him, Larry paced up and down, absorbing what he had learned and trying to weigh his situation. His own cause was virtually hopeless, he had to admit. His sudden appearance in disguise had upset the careful calculations of the Security Service. So it was only natural that Ho F'ang, trying to protect himself, would go to any lengths to prove Richard L. Bliss guilty of treason to China.

In one way or another, Larry thought, evidence of that guilt would be forthcoming. He had been prepared from the start of his mission to sacrifice his life. But it was tormenting to realize how close he had come to success. The information General Hopkins wanted was stored away in his head, but he had no way of relaying it to Washington. He couldn't let himself think about his failure.

Nor could he allow himself to dwell on David. Their reunion had been so brief and unsatisfactory that it was painful to think about the boy.

Richard L. Bliss was probably dead, yet — thanks to his latest perfidy — he had rendered his impersonator helpless.

8

THE SILENCE in the automobile was deafening after the siren stopped screaming, and there was no sound but the roar of the souped-up engine as the car sped down country roads. David knew that he was being taken somewhere east of Peking but decided to ask the grim men of his escort no questions. They had glowered at him during a brief stop at an old barbed-wire-fenced palace when one of the guards had gone inside, perhaps to get instructions. Twice during that halt the boy had started to say something, but had changed his mind and swallowed his words.

Night descended by the time the car screeched to a stop before a steel-mesh gate. Uniformed men surrounded the car, and the driver exchanged a few words with one of them, speaking in such low tones that David couldn't distinguish anything either said. Then suddenly a strong flashlight beam was directed into David's eyes. He blinked, but quickly forced himself to look steadily into the beam so the men wouldn't think he was flinching.

The light was turned off, two guards opened the gate, and the car started forward again, halting once more at the entrance to what appeared to be an expensive private home. David was surprised. He had thought the Security Service men were taking him to prison, but this place didn't even remotely resemble a jail. All the same, the steel-mesh gates and the presence of so many armed guards made him leery.

His escorts conducted him through a pleasant entrance hall into the most handsomely furnished living room the boy had ever seen. Beautiful multicolored silk-screen prints decorated the walls, the thick carpet underfoot was luxurious, and the highly polished furniture gleamed in the glow of softly shaped lamps.

One of the men motioned David to a divan, but he had no sooner seated himself when the door of an adjoining room opened and a burly middle-aged man stood in the frame. The guards immediately jumped to attention, and David stood erect too, raising his arm in the Communist salute, as he had been taught at school.

"Come in, boy," the man said with hearty, somewhat forced joviality. "I understand you're a schoolmate of my nephew."

124

David swallowed hard. "Yes, sir. You must be Ho F'ang Tio Wang."

"Ah, you've heard of me."

The boy found himself in a room with inlaid mosaics of wood on the walls. "Only that you're Ho F'ang-sen's uncle, sir, and that you're important in the government."

Ho F'ang waved him to a chair. "Your guardian holds a post of trust too."

"Yes, sir. I believe he does."

"What do you know about his work?"

"Nothing, sir. Comrade Bliss never talks to me about it." David could see no harm in telling the precise truth. "I asked him once, a few years ago, but he told me it was none of my business."

Ho F'ang laughed. "Still, boys talk. You must know something."

"Comrade Bliss would be angry if I talked out of turn, sir. Just as you wouldn't like it if Ho F'ang-sen boasted about whatever it is that you do."

"Well said, young Heddon." Ho F'ang nodded benignly, but still looked sinister. "We'll talk about these matters after we've taken care of something far more vital to you. What would you like to eat?"

David was surprised anew. "I — Nothing, sir."

"Nonsense! Boys are always hungry! I'll

125

have an almond cake and poppyseed ice cream sent in for you. How does that sound?"

"Wonderful!" Such treats at school were rare, and David's appreciation was genuine.

Ho F'ang went to the door, opened it, and said something to the guard stationed outside. Then, as he returned to his seat, his friendly manner disappeared. "You have something on your mind that's troubling you, boy. What is it?"

David had to think quickly. "Comrade Headmaster Wong will punish me for missing the bus back to the academy, sir. I don't know why I've been brought here, but I wish you would explain to him that it isn't my fault I wasn't at the bus."

Ho F'ang relaxed, like a huge cat ready to pounce. "I've already spoken to him — myself. And he's delighted you're here as my guest. I can give you my own word that you won't be required to copy a chapter from the works of Karl Marx or do extra kitchen duty."

David bit the inside of his cheeks to prevent himself from laughing as he thought of Headmaster Wong cringing, fawning — and agreeing with whatever it was that Ho F'ang had said to him.

"I hear you had something of an argument with young Chen."

"No, sir. I pinned him in a wrestling match and gave him a bloody nose."

"Weren't you afraid of Marshal Chen?" Ho F'ang asked the question casually, but was studying the boy's reactions.

"No, sir. I wasn't fighting the comrade marshal. And it was a fair fight."

"Is that why your guardian came out to the academy to see you?"

David was aware of the obvious trap. "No, sir. He didn't know about it until the comrade headmaster told him. Comrade Bliss comes to visit me occasionally."

"There was nothing strange — or unusual — about this latest visit?"

The boy pretended to reflect. "Not that I can remember, sir."

"What did you discuss?"

"My school grades, mostly. And he was angry because of my fight with the comrade marshal's grandson."

The cat pounced. "You didn't know that Marshal Chen is one of Bliss's protectors?"

David was able to answer in all innocence, "No, sir."

Ho F'ang was obviously disappointed. "Wait for me here," he directed, and left the room abruptly.

A few minutes later a guard arrived with David's food. The cake was delicious, and the ice cream was creamy and smooth, by far the best that David had eaten since leaving the United States.

Ho F'ang came into the room through another door, behind the boy, and David was startled at the sound of his voice.

"You still enjoy eating ice cream and cake in the American style, eh?"

It would be foolish to deny the self-evident. "Yes, sir."

Ho F'ang hadn't expected such an honest reply, and reacted with tolerance. "It's natural to cling to the tastes one develops in early childhood. I find that I'm still partial to the honey cakes of Anhwei Province."

David relaxed a little.

"There are many in this world who cannot or will not give up the ideas they learned in their early years. Do you still believe in the false principles of the imperialist Americans?"

David knew what was expected of him. "No, comrade. I am loyal to the teachings of Marx, and to the ideals of the only true democracy, that of the Chinese people."

Ho F'ang stared hard at him, thick eyelids lowered. "Surely you would like to return to your decadent homeland."

The catechism was similar to the indoctrination courses the boy had been forced to take at the academy. "Never, sir," he said obediently. "China is my homeland."

"And Comrade Bliss, who has treated you as though you were his own son — and has given you the best education available in this great country — is your father?"

The question was tricky, but David knew the proper response. "No, sir. I have only one father — Chairman Mao Tse-tung, who has brought glory to China and made her great."

Ho F'ang seemed satisfied, and leaned back in his chair. "Then you are prepared to serve China, even at the expense of one who has treated you with kindness?"

"I will make any sacrifice." Saying the solemn words here was not the same as repeating them by rote in an academy classroom.

"You will have your chance to prove it. Right now." Ho F'ang stood, and all at once he seemed menacing. "I am taking you to Comrade Bliss. We believe he has been a traitor to China, and we want you to encourage him to speak freely. Knowing that his hours on this earth are numbered, perhaps he will say more to a boy he had hoped to train in his own image than he would to me. Observe him closely, young Heddon, for it may be that he is not what he seems."

A wave of dread washed over David, but he managed to pretend ignorance. "I — don't know what you mean, sir."

"Only members of the presidium perform miracles. They educate the people, give our sons powerful arms, and prepare for the day

129

when we shall rule the whole world. There are no other miracles. I have good cause to believe that it is impossible for Comrade Bliss to be in Peking at this moment, yet you shall stand face to face with him. My mind tells me the man you shall meet is not Comrade Bliss. After you have spoken to him you will report to me anything he says or does that causes you to suspect he is someone other than Comrade Bliss."

Perhaps it was really true, then, David thought, that the man who seemed to be Bliss was really his own father! He felt excited and fearful, happy and worried, all at the same time.

They halted before a second-floor door, which Ho F'ang unlocked and opened. "I've brought you a visitor," he said.

Larry saw his son, and found it virtually impossible to hide his dismay.

David was unable to determine the real identity of the man inside the room, but for the first time believed that he truly might be his father. The boy stood at attention, raising his hand in the clenched fist salute of the Communists. "Comrade Bliss," he said stiffly.

"I'm sorry you've been dragged into this mess, Heddon," Larry replied.

Ho F'ang smiled thinly. "I shall leave you together for a visit," he said.

"While you eavesdrop on a listening device

in another room?" Larry demanded scornfully. "I would discharge anyone in my department who used such crude techniques!"

Ho F"ang was angry. "I thought you'd be pleased to see him. You're ungrateful, Bliss."

Larry kept the initiative he had gained. "And you're afraid of your own shadow, Ho F"ang. Permit us the courtesy of a private conversation."

Ho F"ang had to accept the conditions and depend on a later report from David. But he refused to admit that his prisoner had scored a point at his expense. "If you find it more pleasant to shiver in the cold than stand before a warm log fire, I won't stop you, Bliss. I merely deplore your common

A few minutes later Larry and his son stood in the yard outside the villa, a searchlight trained on them from one of the watchtowers. "We'll walk up and down slowly," Larry said. "Tell me quickly why they've brought you here."

"They think you're a traitor to China and they suspect you aren't Bliss. I'm supposed to tell them anything suspicious you say."

"I see. Tell Ho F"ang I've protested my innocence of wrongdoing. He can prove nothing. I can only thank heaven you aren't directly involved in all this."

"You —you *are* my father. Aren't you?"

"Yes, David."

So many emotions flooded the boy that he couldn't speak.

Larry waited to ease his son's pain, and knowing, too, that they would have only a few minutes together, spoke in a matter-of-fact tone. "You'll be sent back to the academy from here?"

"I guess so. Ho F"ang arranged for me to come here, but I'm sure he'll send me out to the school when he's finished talking with me."

"You won't become involved if you insist to them that I'm Bliss. Now listen carefully. If I can bluff my way out of the spot I'm in I'll find some way to get in touch with you in the next few days. But if you don't hear from me forget that I came to China. Tell yourself I've been dead for a long time."

David discovered he wanted to cry, and was startled. He had spent a long time convincing himself that he felt no love for the father who had abandoned him to the Chinese, but now he was less sure. A man who had transformed himself into the likeness of Bliss and had taken incredible risks obviously cared a great deal for his son.

"Someday," Larry went on, "you may want help. You may want to leave China and return to the United States — "

"I — I haven't even thought about going home. When they first brought me to Peking I dreamed about it, but not any more."

132

"If you still have that dream it can come true. Go to Mao Square. You know where it is?"

"Of course."

"Years ago, before you were born, there was a carp pool in front of the statue of the dowager empress. The railing of the pool still stands, overlooking some bronze plaques with sayings of Mao inscribed on them. Go to the railing and stand there, looking down at the tablets. You may have to go several times before anything happens. But if you're alone — if you make absolutely certain no one is following you — someone who is a friend will approach you. He knows you, although you don't know him. Trust him. Do what he tells you. And perhaps he can smuggle you out of the country." Larry felt hopelessly inadequate, but at least was able to offer some feeble assistance to his son.

"Is this an American agent?" David had read and heard so much about American agents in China that he was impressed. It occurred to him that his father must be a spy too.

"Never mind who he is," Larry said. "Just be wary."

Ho F'ang was beckoning from the entrance to the villa, and they started toward him.

Larry debated with himself whether to say a final farewell to his son, but decided against it. He was afraid he might break down, and he

133

didn't know how David would react either. He remained silent until they drew near to Ho F'ang, then assumed Bliss's remote manner. "I'll pay you a visit at the academy in a few days, Heddon," he said. "Study hard, be obedient, and don't cause any trouble." Turning away quickly, he walked up the stairs to his bedroom-prison, a guard on either side of him.

David accompanied Ho F'ang back to the mosaic-paneled room. "Well?" the Security Service chief asked.

The boy tried to imagine how the real Bliss would have behaved, and made up a story accordingly. "Comrade Bliss was very annoyed, sir," he said. "He told me there had been a mistake, and he called you some uncomplimentary names."

Ho F'ang showed two rows of yellow-white teeth in what he intended as a smile. "I won't ask you to repeat them. Did he mention the Russians to you?"

"No, sir." That much, at least, was true.

"What did he say about his present situation?" Ho F'ang persisted.

"Not much, except that he's sure everything will be cleared up very soon, and that he'll be released." With his father's life at stake, David was finding it surprisingly easy to lie.

Ho F'ang nodded, obviously irritated by the lack of success the confrontation had produced.

"Are you certain the man you've just seen is Comrade Bliss?"

"Positive, sir!" David's reply was emphatic.

The man sighed and ran a hand through his thinning hair. "Very well," he said, his voice unexpectedly resigned. "We must use other means to learn what we want, and you shall have a reward for your loyalty — provided you say nothing — not one word — about your visit here. That will be the great test of your fidelity to the regime. Do I make myself clear?" he added sternly.

"Yes, sir."

"For your sake, I hope so. Now, what reasonable reward would you like?"

David had often imagined himself playing the role of an American secret agent during the years of his enforced stay in China, and now he had his chance. He didn't believe he felt any deep love for his father, but realized at the same time that he desperately wanted to do something for the man — who might otherwise be killed by the Security Service.

Weighing the immediate situation as best he could, he knew that once he was returned to the academy every move he made would be closely supervised. Weeks, even months, might pass before he would be allowed to wander alone in Peking for as long as an hour.

"On a holiday like today, sir, the members

135

of the oldest class at the academy — the boys who will go to a training school for army officers next year — are allowed a special treat. This evening they're seeing the new film about life on collective farms that's playing in the city. They will take a special bus back to the academy at midnight. Ordinarily I'd have to wait two more years for the privilege, but I'd love to see that film, sir."

"I think it can be arranged." Ho F'ang reached into his pocket and handed the boy some coins. "Here. This will pay for your ticket. And I'll notify Headmaster Wong that I've granted you permission. Just remember, young Heddon, tell no one about your visit here!"

"Thank you, sir," David replied with sincerity.

A few minutes later he was seated once more in the automobile with the Security Service guards, who drove him back to Peking at breakneck speed. Although the men did not address David, they were more relaxed than they had been earlier, and occasionally spoke to each other.

The boy pretended to pay no attention to their talk, but learned that they were looking forward to spending a few hours off duty after depositing him at his destination. He hoped they meant what they said. He was gambling that they wouldn't sit with him through the movie or, equally disastrous, turn him over to the dedicated seventeen-year-old boys of the academy's senior class.

Crowds were still heavy in the streets of Peking, so the car's siren wailed, and people scattered, pedestrians and pedicab drivers fleeing toward the sidewalks, the drivers of the few other vehicles hurriedly turning down side streets to avoid the racing Security Service car.

David's tension mounted steadily as the car pulled to a halt in front of the movie theater, tires squealing.

The man sitting in the rear seat, on the right side, climbed out and gestured brusquely.

David's relief was so great that his knees felt weak as he left the automobile. "Good-bye, comrades," he said politely, but the men didn't answer and the car roared off again.

Several pedestrians were staring at the youth who had been delivered to the theater by a carload of guards in the dreaded brown uniforms. David, wanting to call as little attention to himself as possible, walked quickly to the ticket window, then went into the darkened auditorium.

He took a seat in the second row from the rear, on the aisle, and waited until his eyes became accustomed to the gloom. Finally he was able to recognize others in the audience and after a hasty search saw the members of

137

the senior class on the other side of the theater. They were engrossed in the film, and he didn't think they had seen him.

Quietly slipping out of his seat, he made his way back to the street and mingled with the crowds of citizens enjoying their rare holiday from work. Curbing the impulse to run, he forced himself to walk at a sedate pace, occasionally turning his head in what he hoped was a casual manner to see if anyone was following him.

Two soldiers, members of an elite assault infantry regiment, each with a carbine slung over his shoulder, were sauntering a few paces behind him. David walked more rapidly, then looked back again. The soldiers were still there, and his heart hammered in his ears.

He slowed to a crawl, hoping that the infantrymen would pass him. But they remained on his heels, so close that they could reach out and touch him, and he knew that if they had been ordered to follow him he would soon find himself in serious trouble.

If Ho F'ang had directed them to trail him what excuse could he make for leaving the movie he had asked to see as a special treat? Where could he say that he was going now? And what effect might his strange conduct have on his father's welfare?

David shuddered. Some of the older boys at the academy, sons of high officials in a position to know, often boasted that the government had perfected techniques of forcing anyone to tell the complete truth about any given situation. The boy knew himself to be courageous, but was wise enough to realize that his resistance was limited.

He rounded a corner and, as he came onto the Boulevard of Eternal Tranquillity, deliberately halted before a window display of photographs portraying the development of new factories in the great "industrial quadrangle" formed by four teeming cities: Shanghai, Nanking, Nanchang, and Foochow. He was able to catch glimpses of passing pedestrians by watching their reflections in the plate-glass windows of the display, which picked up the light of street lamps.

Finally the two soldiers moved past him. They seemed to be unaware of his presence, and David wondered if he was the victim of his own imagination. He turned to watch them more openly as they were swallowed up by the crowd on the boulevard.

Suddenly a new danger arose. A traffic policeman, immaculate in high boots and a steel helmet, was peering at the boy from his four-foot-high platform in the middle of the boulevard. David knew instantly what had aroused the officer's curiosity. A few children of preschool age were either walking with their parents or were being carried by their fathers.

But there were literally no other boys — or girls — in their teens to be seen anywhere in the throng, and with good reason. As David well knew, adolescents were not free to come and go as they pleased, particularly after dark. Throughout all China they were enrolled in discipline-conscious schools, and always went everywhere in groups, accompanied by their teachers.

A boy of fifteen who seemed to be wandering aimlessly down one of Peking's main thoroughfares after nine o'clock at night inevitably called attention to himself. David wanted to hide, but realized that a failure to behave naturally would mean certain arrest. Acting with a show of confidence far greater than he actually felt, he drifted down the boulevard, moving into the thick of the crowds.

He was so intent on remaining inconspicuous that he walked past Mao Square and didn't realize his error until he had gone a block and a half too far. Impatient with himself, he retraced his steps, occasionally glancing back over his shoulder. To the best of his knowledge, no one was following him.

An icy wind blew through Mao Square, and few pedestrians were loitering there. A young man and woman were strolling slowly, eating roasted watermelon seeds, and several people in the broad-brimmed hats of farmers were staring at the statue of Chairman Mao and the plaques below.

David moved to a spot alone, leaned on the railing, and pretended to be reading the words on the tablets. He felt very nervous.

No one appeared to pay the slightest attention to him. The boy's feet grew numb, and he plunged his hands deep into the pockets of his trousers. A half hour passed, then another, and he thought that soon he would have to leave in order to catch the special bus to the academy.

A pedicab operator circled the square twice and inspected David closely. The boy was aware of the man's scrutiny, and a chill more intense than that caused by the cold crept up his spine.

A short time later a decrepit-looking automobile pulled up at the curb, and a man with a hat pulled low over his forehead beckoned.

David hesitated for an instant, then regained his courage and went to the car.

"Get in," the driver said, and pulled away quickly. "You are young Heddon?"

"Yes, sir."

The driver peered into his rear-view mirror to make certain they weren't being followed. "We've been keeping an eye on you. You've had quite a busy day."

David couldn't be sure that the man wasn't a Security Service agent, and made no reply.

The man chuckled. They drove through the narrow streets of the oldest parts of the city and seemed to be going in circles as they made their way up one winding street and down another. Finally they halted near an alleyway, and the man turned off the engine. "Come along," he said.

David noted that the alley, which was no more than five feet wide, was called the Lane of Jasmine Blossoms. But the odor of rotting garbage in the cobblestones wasn't that of jasmine.

They went to an old apothecary shop. A weather-beaten sign creaked above the entrance, and a dozen dusty bottles and jars of various sizes and colors were the only decorations in the drab window. David followed the man inside.

A dry musty odor assailed his nostrils, and by the light of a single, weak bulb hanging naked from a socket overhead he saw rows of jars, bottles, and jugs lining one wall of the shop. An elderly man with a wispy white beard, a skin that resembled ancient cracked parchment, and a frail body enveloped in an old-fashioned robe of faded embroidered silk was waiting on a customer, a plump woman in tunic and trousers.

The old man looked up and glanced at the newcomers.

"I want to buy some shark's-fin powder for my nephew," the driver of the car said. "He ate too much today, and he has an ache in his stomach."

The plump woman bestowed an amused, motherly smile on David. "Boys of his age always eat too much on holidays."

The aged proprietor coughed. "Is there anything else I can get for you, comrade?"

The woman thought for a moment. "It wouldn't hurt me to buy some blue shark's-fin powder, I suppose. For my headaches."

The old man went to a jar, shook a little of its contents onto a sheet of very thin paper, and deftly folded it so the contents wouldn't spill.

The woman took a long time searching in her pockets for her money and counted it out slowly. Then, her lips moving, she made sure that the old man gave her the right change, which she placed in a shabby wallet of imitation leather.

The driver remained silent and motionless until she was gone. "I've parked the car at the entrance to the lane."

"Then move it," the old man directed crisply, and the change in his tone and manner was remarkable. His voice seemed deeper, firmer, and he moved with the authority of someone much younger. He bolted the door when the driver left, then let down a bamboo blind, which cut off the view from the street. Finally he turned to stare at the boy.

"I — I'm David Heddon."

"I know." The old man switched off the light bulb, leaving the room in total darkness. "Follow me, and try to be quiet."

David, stumbling in the dark, groped down a narrow passage behind the apothecary shop and guessed he was in a corridor that led to living quarters in the rear.

But the old man halted, squatted, and seemed to be groping around the edges of a smooth, square-cut stone underfoot. Eventually he caught hold of a brass ring and lifted the stone. "Go ahead, and don't fall, or you'll break your neck."

David made his way slowly down a flight of steep stairs made of stone. The old man drew the stone into place overhead and then followed.

Suddenly a light was turned on, and David looked around in openmouthed astonishment. He found himself in a modern, comfortably furnished room, complete with easy chairs, lamps, and tables. Only the walls of solid stone were a reminder that he was underground.

His host, walking briskly and showing no trace now of an old man's shuffle, went straight to a telephone on a table at the far side of the cell and pressed a button in its base as he lifted the instrument from its cradle.

"Chuh? Larry Heddon's son has just arrived. . . . Yes, I'm sure. I recognized him from his description. So did D'ang, who brought him here." The old man's deep chuckle reverberated against the stone walls. "We'll soon find out. Send a lookout to the roof, and establish an alert. If he *has* been followed you'll know what to do." He put down the telephone and motioned to a chair.

David's legs felt shaky, and he was glad to sit.

The old man took a chair opposite him, tugged at his beard, and folded his hands in his lap. "Tell me what brings you here, how you knew about going to Mao Square — every detail, no matter how small or minor it may seem to you."

9

DAVID SLEPT for a few hours in a snug underground bedroom and was awakened by someone bringing him breakfast. He was shocked when he saw the brown uniform of a Security Service guard, but the man winked at him, then laughed.

"Don't be alarmed, young one," he said. "We hope to fool others, not you. Li Yu-teh will tell you all you need to know."

Alone again, David was too upset to eat. Had he said too much to the old man? If he was really in the hands of the Security Service, he and his father were seriously compromised.

Again the door opened, and the old man with the wispy beard came into the room, smoking a clay pipe. "You slept well, I hope." He glanced at the tray. "What's this?"

"I — I'm not hungry. The man who brought me the food —"

"That was Chuh. He told me you were

146

startled. Eat, young one. You'll need your strength today." The elderly Chinese bowed. "I haven't introduced myself to you. I am known to some as Li Yu-teh."

His smile was benign, and David forced himself to eat the dish of fried rice and crisp roasted pork.

"The information you brought me about your father last night was valuable — far more valuable than you will ever know. He is a man of great courage, and we will do what we can this morning to save him. As you are his son, you will take part in the plan. In that way, perhaps, we can be of help to him — and to you."

David had so many questions he didn't know which to ask first.

"You are wondering why I interest myself in his welfare and yours. Listen to me, young one. You have been taught many lies about history in your studies at the academy. For years, a great many years, the United States was China's best friend in all the world. The Americans gave us money for our poor, sent us doctors and engineers, and took our sons to be educated at her universities. There are many who have not forgotten America's generosity."

"I didn't tell you I'm a student at the academy," David said.

Li Yu-teh smiled. "We have kept watch over

147

you ever since Richard Bliss first brought you to Peking. I knew Larry Heddon when he was not much older than you, and I have always believed that someday he would find a way to come to China in order to rescue you."

David blinked back unexpected tears. Perhaps he had been wrong to tell himself his father didn't care what happened to him.

"We must move swiftly. I ask you to play a part in our effort because it will be more convenient for everyone. But I can't and won't command you to join. If we should fail, and the authorities should catch you, I'm afraid you'll spend many years in a corrective labor camp — or even in prison."

David's confusion of the past few days suddenly ended, and he knew what he had to do. "I — I want to help."

"Good. As you're finished with your meal, come with me."

The boy followed Li Yu-teh into the room where they had talked the previous night. Several men in Security Service uniforms were talking in low tones, and the one called Chuh rose to his feet and looked questioningly at Li Yu-teh.

"The young one agrees to share our dangers."

David was astonished when the man laughed, shook his hand, and slapped his back.

"We'll find you a uniform," Chuh told him, "and you'll ride with us. Say nothing, and leave everything to us. Li Yu-teh has devised a simple scheme to rescue your father."

The old man smiled wearily. "I've found that simplicity is almost always the most effective weapon to use when dealing with suspicious, complex men. I just wish I could come with you myself, but I'm afraid I'm too old to dress for a masquerade. When you see your father, young one, give him my love. In the meantime, good luck to you."

David started to change into the brown tunic and trousers of a Security Service guard. Still bewildered by the sudden turn of events, he knew only that he was beginning to appreciate the father toward whom he had felt such contempt and indifference.

In midmorning a guard brought Larry his breakfast and watched him impassively as, using his chopsticks numbly, he emptied the wooden bowl. He had no appetite, but didn't know when they would feed him again, so he ate the entire meal. His future seemed hopeless, but he was determined to keep up his strength.

"Tell Ho F'ang," he said as he handed the guard the bowl and chopsticks, "that I demand to see him at once."

The man looked at him contemptuously. "Comrade Ho F'ang returned to Peking last night," he said. "He isn't here."

"When will he be back?"

The guard shrugged, left the room, and locked the door behind him.

The news was discouraging, but no worse than Larry had expected. In all probability Ho F'ang wouldn't see him again until the agent who had murdered Richard L. Bliss was rushed home by plane and came here to confront him. Then, Larry knew, the last act of his tragedy would begin. The Security Service would use every means at its disposal — and it had many — in an attempt to pry information from him.

He walked to the windows, gazed out at the gloomy leaden sky overhead and saw a few stray flakes of snow falling. A real blizzard, he thought, would ground planes coming in from Cambodia — or anywhere else — and might win him a brief respite.

Part of his training had been devoted to preparations for a situation similar to that in which he now found himself. But the real thing bore little resemblance to his schooling. He had been taught to endure long hours of isolation, but nothing could ease the nagging worries that beset him. No instructor could have told him ways to rid himself of the fears he felt for his son's safety.

Larry saw that it was snowing harder now. A steady curtain of thick white flakes was falling, and, as there was little wind, it formed a dense blanket that curtailed his ability to see beyond the electrified fence. The Great Wall was no longer visible, and Larry's feeling of relief increased. He was virtually certain that the plane bringing Bliss's murderer to Peking could not land in this weather. Every hour of added reprieve was a blessing.

There was a mild flurry of activity at the gate, and then a long black sedan moved slowly up the driveway. Ordinarily such luxury cars were used by highest government officials, and Larry wondered if Ho F'ang was returning from the city. A Security Service guard stepped out when the vehicle drew to a halt, and although the man was wearing a short hip-length coat with an upturned collar over his tunic, partly muffling his face, Larry could see that he was shorter than Ho F'ang, and considerably more slender.

Larry lost interest when the man conferred with the sentry who came out of the villa to meet him. But he had nothing better to do, and continued to watch. The newcomer handed the sentry a paper, they talked for a few moments more, and then both disappeared into the building.

Shortly afterward the bedroom door was unlocked and opened, and the guard who had brought Larry his breakfast stood in the frame. "You are leaving immediately," he said, and pointed to the overcoat and hat hanging on a wall peg.

Larry needed no urging to don them, and could see no harm in trying to find out his next destination. "Where am I going?"

The guard did not reply, but indicated with his submachine gun that he wanted the prisoner to precede him.

Larry walked down the stairs to the ground floor, where the sentry and the man from the automobile were waiting. In silence they escorted him to the car.

The engine was running, and two members of the Security Service sat in the front seat, huddling under the upturned collars of their short coats. Another waited on the far side of the back seat, a submachine gun in his hands.

The man in charge went through final formalities with the sentry. "Sign this paper to show that you've released the prisoner," he said, "and here's another for you, which says I've taken him into my custody."

"The red tape grows worse every year," the sentry grumbled.

The transaction was completed, and the man in charge of the operation motioned Larry into the back seat.

The sentry was surprised. "Aren't you going to handcuff him, comrade?"

"That won't be necessary," the other man replied with a contemptuous laugh. "Like all Americans, he's harmless."

A surge of anger welled up in Larry, although he kept his face impassive. Perhaps somewhere on the ride he might have a chance to snatch a submachine gun and shoot his way to freedom. His situation appeared so hopeless that he was willing to take the chance, even though the odds against success were high.

The man in charge climbed in beside him, and the car started off at once, but slowed to a halt again at the gate. There another sentry peered in, and seemed satisfied. "A bad day for a drive," he told the man behind the wheel.

"Ho F'ang never notices weather," was the reply.

Both laughed, the window was rolled up, and the car gained speed rapidly, the guards nestling beneath their high collars.

"Where are you taking me?" Larry asked.

Again there was silence.

It quickly became evident that the driver was not a man who respected hazardous weather conditions. The snow had made the surface of the bumpy road slick, and the car bounced and skidded dangerously as the man behind the wheel continued to increase his speed. The windshield wipers worked steadily, but snow formed on the glass faster than they

153

could brush it away. Luckily there was no other traffic on the road as the automobile lurched from one side to the other.

There must be a lunatic behind the wheel, Larry thought. The car would turn over and kill all of them long before the guards could deliver him to his new prison.

After approximately ten minutes of wild ride the man seated beside the driver raised the visor of his peaked cap, which had been pulled low over his eyes, and turned down the collar of his coat. Twisting around toward the rear, he grinned.

Larry was speechless as he stared at David.

The man who was in charge addressed Larry in English. "You must forgive us for forcing you to endure temporary discomfort, Mr. Heddon, but we have had no choice. Permit me to introduce myself. I am Li Chuh."

Larry recovered the use of his voice. "The son of Li Yu-teh?"

The man bowed, then called to the driver in the local dialect, "Faster, if you can, Pai! And be sure you take the south fork to Anchow when you come to the Revolution monument!"

A feeling of stunned disbelief still enveloped Larry as he looked at the man, then at his smiling son. From what Li Chuh had just said to the driver he gathered that they were heading toward a town southeast of Peking, and had no intention of entering the capital.

David started to explain. "I went to Li Yu-teh last night," he said. "When he heard my story he arranged everything."

"Your son displayed great courage and even greater ingenuity," Li Chuh added. "You have cause to be proud of him, and I know you'll want to hear the whole story — later."

The car skidded wickedly, but the driver managed to keep it on course without lessening speed.

"I'm grateful for the risks that you and these other gentlemen are taking," Larry replied soberly.

"We shall do what we can for you," Li Chuh said, and handed Larry a loaded automatic pistol. "You'll need this, I think. No doubt you were disarmed when Ho F'ang took you into custody."

Larry grinned; he felt more like himself now that he was carrying firearms again. He wouldn't be captured by the Security Service now without putting up a battle.

"Do you have funds?"

"Yes, Ho F'ang let me keep my money."

"How much do you have?" Li Chuh asked.

Larry counted his money. "Twelve thousand yuan."

David, listening intently to the talk of the men, whistled softly.

Li Chuh smiled at the boy and shook his head. "It sounds like a fortune to you, doesn't

155

it? Unfortunately, it isn't enough to see you out of the country." He handed Larry an additional sum in one-hundred-yuan notes. "On the lower levels, most government officials will still take bribes."

Larry didn't reply until he finished counting the money. "You've given me ten thousand yuan. That's very generous."

"A single captain of police or a border guard will gladly relieve you of the whole sum," Li Chuh said with a shrug.

"We're coming into Pochow village!" the driver called.

Li Chuh's manner changed. "Alert station!" he commanded. "David, put on your hat and turn up your collar again. Look straight ahead and say nothing to anyone."

The boy obeyed immediately.

Larry sat back in his seat, resuming his role of Security Service "prisoner." The car slowed to about half its previous speed, but driving was still dangerous. Through the steam-coated windows he could see small wooden houses, and behind them, a glimpse of a curving pagoda roof.

"The police station is directly ahead," the driver warned.

Li Chuh picked up his submachine gun from the floor and held it ready for instant use. The other "guards," David included, followed his example.

Suddenly the driver slammed on his brakes and the car barely inched forward at a snail's pace. He cursed softly, under his breath.

"What's wrong?" Li Chuh demanded.

"A farmer's bullock cart is in front of us," the driver said, "and I can't pass him on this narrow road. Shall I use the siren?"

"No! We can't afford to call attention to ourselves when we're less than a block from the local police station." Li Chuh strained to see out of his window as he again addressed himself to Larry. "If an alarm has been given and the road is blockaded, Mr. Heddon, you and David will have to run for it. We'll do what we can to cover you."

Larry nodded and took a firm grip on the new automatic. Pochow was only fifteen miles from Peking, far too close for comfort, and in this frightful weather it wouldn't be possible to go far on foot.

A policeman wearing a fur hat and ear muffs, heavy coat, and thick mittens was standing outside the modern two-story police headquarters. A few feet from him, partly protected from the elements by a canvas cloth, was his motorcycle. He was cold, miserable, and bored, but the approaching automobile, moving at a crawl, provided him with a diversion.

He looked hard at it, recognized the uniforms of the Security Service, and stood at

157

attention, raising his hand in the Communist salute.

Li Chuh and the man at the opposite side of the rear seat returned the greeting.

David laughed when the policeman failed to follow them.

But Li Chuh quickly reproved him. "When Peking gives a general alarm," he said, "that fellow will remember us and the route we're taking. Too bad. We're fortunate, though, that my father took such accidents into account when he planned our journey."

The bullock cart turned off into a snow-laden side road, and the automobile roared as it suddenly shot ahead again.

"What do you have in mind?" Larry asked. "Where do we go from here?"

"Our resources are limited," Li Chuh replied, "but we shall provide you with the best transportation facilities available to us. The great problem, of course, is to prevent the authorities from finding you, Mr. Heddon. As you're a Caucasian, you'll be conspicuous everywhere. The militia of every province and the police of every town will be looking for an American. We thought of having you pretend you're a Russian — "

"Impossible," Larry interrupted. "I don't speak the language. And even if I did, Russians aren't welcome in China these days."

"That sums up the situation." Li Chuh wiped the rear window and looked out to see if they were being followed. "Of course David looks sufficiently Oriental to travel anywhere without arousing suspicions. And although he's undoubtedly been reported as missing from the Sun Yat-sen Academy, no one — not even Ho F'ang — can be positive that you'll be traveling together. So he'll have to act as your eyes and ears."

"Fair enough," Larry said thoughtfully. "Do you have any particular escape route to suggest?"

"We shall do more than suggest — for at least a part of your journey." Li Chuh offered no details at the moment. "I'm afraid you won't like this, but we have no ships available to take you out of China by sea. Also, the government's shore-patrol junks are too efficient. We've lost several good men that way in the past two years."

Larry understood the significance of the remark and realized the enormity of the task that awaited him. He and David would be forced to travel through hundreds of miles of hostile territory in the hope that they could cross the border of the British crown colony of Hong Kong, far to the south. The very idea of undertaking such a venture was staggering.

"I'll have to keep Bliss's identity papers,"

he said, "and hope that any official who wants to see them is careless or hasn't received instructions from the Security Service." He paused for a moment. "What will become of you — and these gentlemen?"

The men laughed. "Don't worry about us," Li Chuh told him. "Within a very few hours we'll be safe and sound in Peking."

"But surely a search will be made for this car!" Larry protested.

Li Chuh smiled faintly. "For everyone's protection, I can't tell you too much. However, to put your mind at ease, we shall resume our public identities soon after we part company with you. My silent friend," he continued, gesturing toward the man on Larry's left, "has the right to possess a car such as this. He has a valid reason for making a trip into the country outside Peking, and the position of trust he holds is such that no one will think of connecting him — or his car — with Richard L. Bliss."

Larry tried to get a better look at the man, but he continued to avert his face. Perhaps it was best that a foreigner who might be recaptured not know too many details about the people who were helping him. It was enough, Larry realized, that a man of very high rank in the Red Chinese government was sufficiently disillusioned with the Communist regime to help an American trying to leave China after performing an espionage mission.

The storm became more intense. The temperature was still dropping, the efficiency of the car's heater was reduced, and the numbing cold added to everyone's tension.

The car turned onto a manor road but the driver continued to maintain a suicidal speed of more than fifty miles per hour, clinging with all his strength to the wheel. Thirty minutes passed, then another fifteen, and Larry, whose sense of direction was sharp, knew only that they were somewhere southeast of Peking.

"Soon," the driver said at last.

Li Chuh reached into the pocket set on the inside of the door and drew out an ordinary gray tunic, trousers, and cap. "Change into these things," he told David, "and give me your Security Service uniform."

David obeyed, taking care not to jostle the driver's arm.

"I also have new identity papers for you," Li Chuh told him, leafing through them. "Learn your new name, and don't forget that the authorities will also be searching for Richard Bliss's runaway ward." A sudden thought struck him. "Are you familiar with the Hopeh dialect?"

"Yes, sir," David said.

"He's known it since he was a very small boy," Larry added.

"Excellent," Li Chuh said. "Speak nothing else. You'll draw too much attention to yourself if you use Mandarin. Ah, here we are."

The car pulled to a halt and stood, its engine still idling. Larry and David followed Li Chuh into the bitter cold after hastily shaking hands with the others in the car, and stood shivering in what appeared to be a deserted, blizzard-swept wheat field. Off to the left was a stand of catalpa trees and, beyond it, a few of the so-called "paper trees" found everywhere in China, their branches bare.

"I'll relieve you of the submachine gun," Li Chuh said to the boy, and took the weapon.

David was unhappy. "I know how to use it," he said. "We had practice at the academy every week."

Larry shook his head. "You'll have to prove your marksmanship with something else, son. Only Ho F'ang's people and the assault infantry use these guns."

Li Chuh pointed toward the right. "Go three hundred yards in a straight line," he said. "There you'll find someone waiting to guide you on the next leg of your journey. I wish I could see you to him safely, but it is too dangerous for us to stay here. Good-bye, David. Mr. Heddon, I wish you well. May we meet again when China is a free land." He glided

162

away swiftly, looking like a phantom as the storm hid him from sight.

Father and son could hear but not see the car start up again and move off. Then there was silence, eerie and frightening, with no sound but the howling of the wind that was gathering force.

Larry put one hand on David's shoulder and gripped his automatic with the other. "Let's get going," he said quietly, and they started off together through the snow.

10

IN PLEASANT WEATHER a walk of only three hundred yards would have taken no more than a few minutes. But with the blizzard still gaining strength, Larry proceeded cautiously. Even Arctic explorers, he knew, sometimes lost their bearings in storms this fierce.

David's teeth chattered, but he made no complaint as he trudged on, the snow beneath his boots squeaking with each step. So much had happened since he had gone to Li Yu-teh's apothecary shop that he still felt dazed. But he was neither frightened nor upset. He was conscious of the solid steady pressure of his father's hand on his shoulder, and all was right with the world.

Suddenly Larry halted and put his lips close to his son's ear. "There's a house — a shack, really — straight ahead."

David heard a clicking sound as his father removed the safety catch from the automatic.

They started forward again, moving still more slowly.

A deep male voice cut through the storm. "Who is out there?"

"Friends, comrade!" Larry shouted, speaking in the same Hopeh dialect.

There was no reply, but as they came closer they saw a burly middle-aged man covering their approach with a rifle. Not until they were a scant five paces from him did he seem satisfied with their identity and lower the weapon.

"Come aboard," he said, his tone inhospitable. "I thought you'd never arrive, but now that you're here help me shove off before the water turns into solid ice and freezes me to the landing."

Larry and David were surprised to see that he was actually standing on the broad deck of a wooden barge. Amidships was the wooden shack that served as both a dwelling and pilot-house. It was surrounded by large drums of gasoline, and both fore and aft, under thick covers of water-repellent cotton, was the barge's cargo.

Father and son climbed aboard, and Larry smiled as he gestured in the direction of the water. "The Grand Canal!" he exclaimed.

The barge owner, badly in need of a shave, tugged at the thick woolen scarf wrapped around his neck and handed each of them a

165

long pole. "Of course it's the canal," he snapped. "In the names of the ten thousand devils that inhabit the netherworld, did you think it was the Yellow Sea?"

In spite of the unpleasant greeting, Larry felt enormously reassured, and marveled at the cunning of Li Yu-teh. The Grand Canal was a vast man-made waterway more than two thousand years old that ran parallel to the seacoast from a point near Peking, through some eight hundred miles of farmlands, terminating near the city of Hangchow, south of Shanghai. Once a main artery of traffic, it had gradually fallen into disrepair, and when Larry had last visited China silting had made parts of it unusable.

But the Reds had put thousands of political prisoners to work digging the channel again, and the entire length was now navigable and was utilized principally for the transportation of farm products from regions of plenty to famine-stricken areas. The canal looped around major cities, cutting through none of them, and was the last place in China that Ho F'ang would search for an escaped American. No one who was in a hurry traveled on the Grand Canal.

The barge owner glowered at his guests, then went to the broad stern, where a battered gasoline engine was located. After several attempts he managed to start it, and it sputtered in protest as it warmed up.

The man made his way back to the starboard side, amidships, and pointed toward the shack. "I steer from there," he said. "When I give you the signal, shove off." He disappeared into the shack, and a moment later shouted.

Larry jumped to the shore and untied a line fixed to a stake driven into the ground, then leaped onto the deck again. He and David used all their strength to push the cumbersome craft away from the shore. At last the barge started to move, and they leaned on their poles, gasping for breath, just as coolies had done since time immemorial.

Ice had formed a crust near the bank, but the bargeman steered out toward the center of the canal, where the water was flowing more freely, running at a very slow rate of speed from north to south. It was fed by rivers moving down from the hills to the west, and as always Larry was impressed by the ingenuity of ancient China's architects.

Snow stung the faces of father and son, cold numbed their hands and feet, and when the barge began to crawl smoothly down the canal Larry gestured toward the shack. "We haven't been invited," he said, "but let's go inside."

The interior was surprisingly comfortable.

A wood fire crackled in a gasoline drum that was placed, for safety's sake, in a pan of sand, smoke escaping through a crude funnel of tin that was set in the roof and served as a chimney. The only furniture consisted of several clumsy, homemade chairs of wood tied together with thongs, and in one corner were a pile of reed mats and blankets that evidently served as beds. The bargeman was perched on a stool, staring out through a windshield of heavy glass that was cracked in several places. He could see no further than his prow, but did not turn as his guests came into the warm cabin.

"The boy," he said, "will feed the fire with wood and the engine with gasoline. I will show him how to pour in the gasoline."

"I know how to operate an engine," David said.

The barge owner pretended he hadn't heard. "Yang will show him," he said. "On Yang's ship, there is only one master. You," he added to Larry, "will relieve me at the tiller. Care must be taken to stay on the right side of the canal so we don't collide with barges coming in the opposite direction."

Larry knew that signs of respect were very important to such a man. "We will gladly take instruction from Yang," he said solemnly. "Now, let me present ourselves to Yang. We are —"

"Never mind!" the bargeman shouted. "I don't want to know your names — or anything about you. It is enough that I am carrying wheat and beans to Shanghai — and that you will help me on the voyage."

"It is enough," Larry repeated, closing the subject. It was best not to volunteer information or, for that matter, inquire how Li Yuteh had acquired the man's services.

"If you're hungry," Yang said indifferently, "there is food in the box behind the woodpile."

David immediately brightened, but his father silenced him with a frown. Etiquette, always important in China, was essential when people were forced to live in close quarters on a barge that moved so slowly. "We will wait until Yang is hungry," Larry said. "Then we will eat together."

A deep, gruntlike noise indicated the bargeman was pleased.

The storm continued to rage through the long hours of the day, and Yang remained glued to his post, apparently feeling no discomfort or hunger. David became ravenous, and his boredom made him restless. There was nothing for him to do except throw sticks onto the fire from time to time, and the exhilaration he had felt earlier slowly faded.

Further travel became impossible shortly after nightfall, as the barge was not equipped with lights. Yang took David to the engine,

169

showed him how to fill its battered gas tank, and returned with the boy to the cabin just as Larry completed the task of making the clumsy craft secure for the night. For a few minutes all three huddled around the gasoline-drum stove, and at last Yang went to his box of food supplies.

Dinner consisted of coarse-ground millet bread, a trifle stale, chunks of cold pork, and a puree of highly seasoned soybeans that might have been palatable if served hot. Larry almost gagged on the stuff, but David was so hungry that he scraped his wooden bowl clean. Then, when the unsatisfactory meal was finished, Yang produced his most precious possession, a transistor-powered radio, which he carefully and lovingly unwrapped from a protective covering of padded cotton.

One of the Peking radio stations was playing martial music that Yang seemed to enjoy as, sitting cross-legged on a frayed reed mat, he stuffed and lighted a clay pipe.

Larry had to raise his voice in order to make himself heard above the blaring trumpets and crashing cymbals. "We must make financial arrangements for our transportation!" he shouted.

Yang puffed calmly on his pipe. "Your fare to Peking has been paid," he replied.

Larry felt encouraged. Many men as poor

170

as Yang would have greedily accepted another fee.

"But you work for your meals," the surly bargeman added.

"Of course." Larry hesitated for an instant, then proceeded delicately. "How do you obtain your food supplies?"

"I buy them at villages that we pass."

"In that case, perhaps you will do me the honor of allowing me to pay for loaves of wheat-flour bread, whole-grained rice, and strips of beef." Larry could still taste the revolting soybean dish.

Yang's dark eyes gleamed, but his face remained impassive. "If you wish," he said, refusing to admit that he looked forward to the more expensive diet he himself couldn't afford.

The band music on the radio stopped for a newscast, and after the broadcast of several items on international affairs another speaker said, "Attention, all peace-loving patriots! With the help of evil conspirators, an enemy of the Chinese people has escaped from the protective custody of government officials who were bringing him to justice!"

David stiffened.

Larry glanced surreptitiously at Yang, who continued to puff on his pipe, giving no indication that he had even heard the news bulletin.

"He is an American imperialist," the announcer continued, "who won the confidence of the people's representatives but has betrayed China. This man, who is called Bliss, is believed to be hiding somewhere in the Peking area." He went on to give an accurate description of the escaped prisoner.

David became panicky, but his father's calm reassured him. Larry seemed to be paying no heed to the voice.

"Attention, all comrades!" the announcer continued. "A reward of five thousand yuan will be paid to any patriot who gives the authorities information that will lead to the arrest of the revisionist criminal, Bliss. It is requested that he be captured alive so that he can be forced to reveal the identities of the traitors who aided him in his attempt to flee from the people's justice."

Larry was relieved to learn that Li Chuh and his companions had not been caught. Whatever their means, they had slipped back into their normal daily routines.

"Remember, citizens, a reward of five thousand yuan will be paid for information that will lead to the arrest of this dangerous enemy. Long live Mao Tse-tung! Long may the People's Republic flourish!"

Military band music again flooded the cabin of the barge.

Yang's face was half concealed behind a

cloud of smoke, but Larry tried to gauge his reaction to the news. At best, the bargeman earned one thousand yuan in return for a year of hard labor, and the sum of five thousand undoubtedly seemed like a vast fortune to him. No matter how much Li Chuh had paid him, he might find the temptation of the reward irresistible. Certainly he knew the identity of the man sitting only four feet from him; the announcer's description had been painfully clear and precise.

Larry wondered whether to offer the man a bribe to keep quiet, but decided the move would be unwise. Yang had been emphatic in his demand that his passengers refrain from revealing their names to him. Hence there was at least a chance that, for whatever his reasons, he might refuse to betray the man and boy who were now in his power. On the other hand, if he chose to alert the authorities, a bribe would not deter him. He could accept the money, and then go to the police.

There appeared to be no real choice, and Larry finally made up his mind. He would accept the bargeman's attitude at face value, and would maintain a discreet silence.

After listening to the band music for another half hour or more, Yang suddenly snapped off the radio and wrapped it again in its covering. "We begin our voyage again at dawn," he said. "It is time now to sleep."

173

Without further ado he removed his shoes, stretched out on his mat, and pulled a tattered blanket over him.

A meaningful nod from Larry indicated that David was to do the same. The boy obeyed reluctantly, but felt reassured when he saw his father drag a mat to a place directly in front of the cabin door. A few moments later he heard a faint but distinct clicking sound beneath Larry's blanket, and knew that his father had removed the safety catch from his automatic.

If Yang harbored any notions of sneaking ashore during the night and giving the alarm, he would have to climb over Larry Heddon's body — and would be shot to death for his pains.

David believed himself wide awake and tense, but the knowledge that his father was keeping watch lulled him and he soon dropped off to sleep.

When the first streaks of dawn appeared in the sky Yang was awake. Larry sat up too, first carefully stowing away his automatic, and they aroused David. All three washed in canal water they boiled in an iron pot over the fire and then ate a breakfast of the same food that had comprised their menu the previous evening.

The storm had ended during the night. Larry

cast off, and the voyage was resumed at sunrise. Snow lay heavily on both banks of the Grand Canal and the hills beyond, and chunks of ice floated lazily down the water toward the south. But a brilliant sun climbed higher in a cloudless sky, and its mere appearance dissipated some of the anxiety that both Larry and David had felt after hearing the broadcast.

Larry wanted to know what the authorities were saying today about his escape and, particularly, find out whether an alarm had also been given for David. But Yang apparently regarded his radio as too valuable for daytime use, and it might be a blunder to ask him to turn it on.

The fact that Yang had not tried to sneak off during the night was not significant. They hadn't anchored near a village, and he might be waiting for an appropriate time during the day to notify the police that the wanted man was on board his barge. Larry knew he would have to remain alert during the day.

In midmorning they encountered another barge, laden with machinery of some sort. It was traveling in the opposite direction. Yang pulled a rope that rang a small, chiming bell in greeting, and the operator of the other craft answered with a friendly toot on an old automobile horn. Larry made himself inconspicuous, sitting on his mat so he couldn't be seen

175

from the other barge. Yang gave no sign that he was conscious of the act or its significance.

Less than an hour later they saw a patrol of mounted soldiers off to their left. The squad, numbering about a dozen men, was fanned out over a wide front, riding slowly in the same direction that the barge was moving. Larry believed it almost certain they were searching for him, and immediately dropped his hand into his pocket to clasp his automatic.

But the leader of the unit, a young officer whose only distinguishing insignia was a brass medallion pinned to his collar, glanced once in the direction of the barge and showed no interest in it. An older, more experienced officer might have insisted that Yang anchor and submit to an inspection of his craft. But the young man had not been given orders to search barges for the fugitive, Larry thought, and therefore the idea of hailing Yang did not occur to him.

Grateful for the respite, Larry relaxed again. At noon, however, he became alert once more when Yang docked the barge at a wharf only a stone's throw from a village of about thirty houses that was dominated by a large and unattractive building of corrugated iron. This, in all probability, was the commune hall where the residents of the hamlet and farmers of the nearby area were required to eat all their meals, listen to regularly scheduled speeches by government representatives, and send their children to school.

Yang announced that he intended to buy food and made no comment when Larry gave him twenty yuan to purchase supplies more appetizing than his own ordinary, crude fare. Yang pocketed the money, then announced flatly, "The boy will come with Yang to carry firewood."

Larry was torn between an urge to protest and a desire to preserve a façade of normalcy. The request seemed reasonable enough on the surface, and the admission of a fear that Yang intended to use David as a hostage might give the bargeman ideas. A quick decision was necessary, and Larry said, "If you wish." He would watch them through the windshield, and if he saw anything out of the ordinary taking place, would follow them immediately.

As they went ashore he unwrapped Yang's radio and, keeping a sharp lookout, switched it on, making certain he kept the volume low. He turned the dial slowly as he searched for a newscast. One Peking station was broadcasting a lecture on crop rotation, and on another a speaker was asking for volunteers to help build a new iron foundry in Tsinan, the capital of neighboring Shantung Province. "All citizens should respond patriotically to this call," the voice declared. "If the response is too

177

small, office workers and other city parasites will be drafted for eight weeks of labor."

Yang and David had reached the village, and while the man disappeared into a hut David lingered in the snow outside. He turned once in the direction of the barge, certain that his father was watching, and Larry's fleeting smile was reassuring.

Larry finally tuned in a news broadcast, and after a time heard, "A boy of fifteen summers who was the ward of the vile traitor, Bliss, has disappeared from Peking. It is feared that the criminal Yankee has murdered him. Therefore the reward for information leading to the capture of Bliss has now been doubled to ten thousand yuan."

He snapped off the radio and, still keeping an eye on David, who was now walking to another hut with Yang, tried to weigh the latest newscast. The most important fact to be gleaned from it was that Ho F'ang now knew that David was missing. In all probability there had been a flurry of telephone calls after the boy had failed to return to his dormitory at the academy. But the head of the Security Service could only guess what had become of him. Thanks in part to David's own avoidance of surveillance, in part to the cleverness of Li Yu-teh, the authorities didn't know where to begin their search for the boy.

178

One portion of the broadcast had been ridiculous gibberish, and Larry felt sure that Ho F'ang knew it. The authorities might suspect that Bliss and David were making a joint effort to escape, but there were no grounds for the charge that the "American traitor" had murdered his ward. Ho F'ang was deliberately trying to paint as black a portrait of the fugitive as he could. If the people developed intense hatred for Bliss, it would be relatively easy to obtain a conviction at a public trial — provided, of course, that the Security Service managed to find and capture its quarry.

Yang emerged from the hut, carrying several packages and a wooden pail, which he handed to David. They exchanged a few words, then went on to another house. So far the bargeman's food shopping expedition appeared legitimate.

After another twenty minutes of shopping Yang and David returned to the barge, the boy carrying most of the items they had purchased. Larry hastily replaced the radio in its protective covering, but took care not to show the relief he felt. Perhaps Yang could be trusted, although it was too soon to tell. It was unlikely that there was more than one police officer in the village, and the real test would come when they reached a town with a full complement of police.

The voyage was resumed, the barge propelled as much by the running waters of the canal as by its decrepit engine. It was ironic, Larry thought, that even though a vast manhunt was in progress he was only two or three hours from Peking by automobile. And at the barge's present rate of speed several days would pass before they reached Shantung Province. He hated to guess how long the whole voyage might last.

At least the meals would improve. In addition to rice, white bread, and a package of fresh green noodles, Yang had bought a large fish that, when grilled, would provide the main course for two meals. And it would be a luxury to drink tea instead of boiled canal water.

Early in the afternoon several single-engined planes roared overhead, moving south at a height of no more than one thousand feet. They were painted gray and yellow, the colors of the small Chinese air force, but carried no insignia on their sides. Larry, gazing up at them from the cabin as he half crouched behind the windshield, wondered if they were Security Service aircraft taking part in the search for him.

Less than thirty minutes later his worst fears were confirmed. A gray and yellow helicopter showed up from the direction of Peking, swooped down, and hovered directly overhead at about five hundred feet. Yang promptly ordered Larry to steer the barge and went out onto the open deck to move several drums of gasoline.

David turned to his father anxiously. "Is he signaling to them?"

"I don't know," Larry was half squatting behind the windshield so he couldn't be seen from the air. "Watch every move he makes, son."

"I am. What'll we do if he lets them know you're here?"

"One step at a time, David." Larry didn't want to alarm his son, but knew there would be bloodshed if the authorities discovered his hiding place.

Yang returned to the cabin, making no comment as he took control of the barge again. A few moments later the helicopter rose higher and disappeared in the direction of Peking.

In the silence that followed, David was troubled. Larry felt uneasy too. Ten minutes passed, then another ten, and suddenly the quiet was broken by the steady hum of an approaching diesel-powered boat.

Yang calmly raised his head and turned to the boy. "You will tell me your name now."

"Chang," David replied, using the name on his false identity papers. Perhaps it wasn't accidental that Li Yu-teh had used his late mother's maiden name.

Yang nodded but said no more.

Larry looked out through the windshield

181

and saw, coming straight toward them at high speed, a steel-hulled boat with machine guns mounted fore and aft. On its deck stood seven or eight armed men — all of them wearing Security Service uniforms.

Before Larry could speak or act Yang took charge. "Hide under the wheat bags near the stern, where they are piled highest," the bargeman told him. "Hurry, and no matter what happens, don't make a sound."

Larry started toward the door. "Come on, David."

"No," Yang said. "The boy will stay with me."

In one to two minutes the boat would draw alongside, and there was no time to argue. If Larry didn't trust Yang he had only one alternative, that of opening fire with his automatic when the Security Service men approached. Aware that there were too many of them for him to win such a battle, he realized that he had to put his faith in the enigmatic bargeman.

He went out into the open, using the shack as a shield to hide him from the guards on the high-speed boat. He ran aft, lifted the tarpaulin, and made a place for himself among the cold, damp burlap bags. He took care to keep one small corner of the covering raised so he could see as well as hear what was happening. The boat was coming still closer, and when the

182

bargeman and David came onto the deck Larry took his automatic from his pocket and peered down the barrel at Yang. If the man tried to give him away he would be the first to die.

One of the Security Service men made fast a line, joining the boat and the barge, and the others leaped onto the broad deck of the clumsy craft. One, who wore a red star on his visored hat, shouted, "Stop your engine!"

Yang was neither cowed nor flustered. "It costs much money to start the engine after turning it off. Who will pay for the extra oil and petrol that I use?"

The reply was typical of the poor, who had to save their yuan zealously, and the officer had no desire to start an interminable argument. "Then turn it down to an idle," he ordered.

"See to it, Chang," the bargeman told David.

The boy was unaccustomed to the new name, and when he failed to respond instantly Yang cuffed him with such force across the side of the face and head that he fell to the deck with a hard thump. The bargeman aimed a vicious kick at him, but he rolled over, avoiding the blow. Leaping to his feet, he ran aft and shifted the gears of the throbbing engine to neutral.

Larry, watching the scene from beneath the tarpaulin, had to curb his own anger. Yang's realistic play-acting had been unnecessarily brutal, and a trickle of blood had appeared at one corner of David's mouth.

183

"My nephew," the bargeman told the Security Service guards complacently, "is a lazy little brute."

The officer nodded as David rejoined the group. Such harsh treatment of a boy was both natural and commonplace, and no one seemed surprised.

"Show me your identity papers," the officer said.

"Get them, Chang."

"Where are they, honored uncle?" David asked, playing his part to the hilt in spite of his pain.

"In the kettle, where I always keep them!" Yang roared, then turned to the uniformed men with a shrug. "The beast is also stupid."

When David returned with the documents, which the government required everyone over seven years of age to carry, the gash at the side of his mouth was bleeding freely. But he made no attempt to wipe away the blood. If he produced a handkerchief from his pocket he would reveal his true status; nephews of poverty-stricken barge owners didn't carry handkerchiefs. He didn't dare wipe his mouth on the sleeve of his tunic either, as he had no idea how many days or even weeks might pass before he could change to clean clothes. And bloodstains on a sleeve would be too convenient a means of identifying him on the flight.

As he had already learned from his father, anonymity was their best protection.

Larry, observing every move and gesture from his hiding place, concluded that Yang had no intention of telling the guards he was concealing a fugitive on board. The bargeman's surprising attitude was heartening, in spite of the blow he had given David.

"These papers seem to be in order," the officer said. "Now we'll search this pigsty."

"Why is that necessary, comrade?" Yang demanded, his tone surly.

The officer drew himself to his full height. "An enemy of the People's Republic is hiding from justice."

Yang's bellow of coarse laughter carried on the cold air across the canal. "Not even the worst of China's enemies would hide with the mice among the soybean bags, comrade!"

The officer relented slightly, and smiled. "Probably not," he agreed. "But we must do our duty." He waved his men toward the cargo stored on the forward part of the barge.

The Security Service guards made a perfunctory search, lifting the tarpaulins here and there as several prodded the bags with the butts of rifles. Then the officer went forward to poke among the bags with his sword.

Yang was at his side instantly. "Don't cut my burlap!" he shouted. "It's expensive!"

The officer sighed. "Show a little respect for a representative of the people."

"We who toil are the true representatives of the people!" Yang spoke rapidly as the officer halted only a few feet from Larry's hiding place and lifted the tarpaulin there with his sword. "Comrade Mao said so in his great speech at the sports arena. I know, because I was there myself, and I heard him. If you harm my property I'll complain to the presidium."

Larry burrowed deeper under two heavy bags of wheat. An insect crawled across the bridge of his nose and down his cheek, but he didn't dare raise his arm to brush it away for fear of moving one of the sacks above him.

Suddenly he saw something bright no more than an inch or two from his face, and realized the officer was jabbing at random with his sword.

"Honored uncle," David said, trying desperately to create a diversion, "should I get these gentlemen some tea?"

"Must you ask, idiot?" Yang shouted. "Bring them some of the cold pork we had two days ago, too. And some crusts of the millet bread, if they aren't stale."

The officer shuddered and quickly decided to bring his investigation to a close. "Back to the boat at once!" he told his men sharply.

Yang sounded genuinely aggrieved. "You're too grand for my hospitality!"

The officer wanted no more to do with a man too ignorant to fear or respect the dreaded Security Service. "Here," he said, scribbling on a pad he took from a pocket and tearing off a sheet of paper.

Yang handed the paper to David. "You read it," he ordered. "My eyes have been bothering me lately."

The officer smiled condescendingly.

David, face and jaw aching from the blow he had received, had to pretend he didn't know that Yang could not read. "This is a pass," he said, "that will permit us to proceed beyond a check point on the canal."

"It's three miles from here," the officer said as he returned to the boat. "Don't lose that paper or you'll be held up for days."

The boat moved off in the direction of Peking. Yang watched until it disappeared from sight, then lifted the tarpaulin. "You're safe now," he called, "but you'll have to hide again at the check point." Not waiting for a reply, he put his engine in gear and sauntered off to the cabin.

David waited for his father to emerge and rejoin him. The cut on the side of the boy's mouth still throbbed, but one more crisis had been overcome. Now they knew they could rely on Yang in whatever emergencies might lie ahead.

11

THE BARGE sailed down the Grand Canal at a leisurely speed, averaging no more than thirty miles per day. On the surface, life was tranquil and even boring, but Larry remained alert, always ready for trouble, and David did not allow himself to relax either. Yang continued to be surly and uncommunicative, rarely smiled, and held himself aloof.

On the eighth day of the journey the batteries of the transistor radio failed, cutting the trio off from the outside world. Larry offered the bargeman money for new batteries, but none was available in the villages and small towns they passed. Yang explained that he wouldn't be able to buy replacements until they reached Shanghai, his destination.

They saw no newspapers either, so Larry knew nothing of new developments in Ho F'ang's search for him. The pursued, like the pursuers, were groping blindly in the dark.

On the tenth day, low-flying planes passed overhead for the last time. Thereafter nothing marred the serenity of the voyage. No Security Service patrols disturbed the travelers, and the only soldiers they ever saw were small militia units conducting training maneuvers. For all practical purposes the two men and the boy were in a remote world of their own, sailing down the Grand Canal west of Tsinan and east of Kaifeng. Not until they floated through the suburbs of Chinkiang, only a few miles from the great city of Nanking, did they see tall factories, automobiles, and trucks.

This emergence into the twentieth century was a reminder that the safety Larry and David had been enjoying was an illusion. They would have to abandon the refuge of the barge when Yang left the Grand Canal and made his way up a river that would take them into China's largest city, Shanghai.

On the twenty-second night of the journey, after traveling almost eight hundred miles, Larry broached the subject. For supper they shared noodles, bean sprouts, and chunks of pork that had been bought the previous day, and as they were finishing their meal Larry broke the silence.

"When do we reach Shanghai?" he asked.

"If all goes well, after sundown tomorrow," Yang replied.

The Security Service maintained its largest detachment in the great metropolis, and thousands of policemen and soldiers were stationed there too. A Caucasian whose escape had been publicized would be picked up almost immediately if he entered the heart of the city.

"Did those who paid for our passage," Larry asked carefully, "tell you whether friends will meet us in Shanghai?"

Yang shrugged, then reached for the last piece of pork in the kettle.

Larry tried wording the question another way. "Have arrangements been made for our reception?"

The bargeman calmly licked his fingers. "Tomorrow morning we reach the Whangpoo branch of the great Yangtze River. We will see thousands of houses, as numerous as the fish in the sea. We will pass steel mills and flour mills — "

"Yes, and manufacturing plants of many kinds," Larry interrupted, hoping to cut short a ponderous lecture on the diversity of Shanghai's industry.

Yang stubbornly insisted on speaking his mind in his own way. "Ching Ke-yeh, who is the cousin of my wife, lives in Shanghai."

Larry waited, listening intently now, his annoyance vanishing.

"Ching Ke-yeh worked in a rubber plant

that made tires for automobiles." Yang sipped scalding tea from a cracked earthernware mug. "Life was very hard for him. Living in Shanghai is expensive, and he had many mouths to feed. Ching was ambitious. From his childhood he wanted fine silks and a beautiful house."

David thought it odd that the bargeman should be talking so freely, and stopped daydreaming to listen carefully too.

"Ten years ago Ching joined the Communist party. Now he is the assistant manager of a cotton plant. His wife wears silks and thinks she is too good for her husband's family. Ching is a very patient man. Sometimes he is too patient. He should make her show respect for his cousins. In a people's democracy a poor bargemaster should be treated as the equal of a Communist who is the assistant manager of a cotton mill."

Larry nodded, taking care to remember every word. Obviously Yang was trying to warn him.

The bargeman gulped the rest of his tea, wiped his mouth on his sleeve, and pointed toward the mats. "Tomorrow," he said, "will be a long day."

Larry and David stretched out on their mats, thinking about Yang's story, but it was difficult for them to concentrate. In another twenty-four hours they would be forced to leave this sanctuary and resume their flight.

The Chinese boasted that Shanghai, with a population of more than eleven million, had become the world's largest city. Regardless of whether this claim to size was accurate or not, it was certainly one of the ugliest cities on earth. The barge, sweeping at the fastest speed it had attained on its voyage, thanks to the strong current of the Whangpoo, passed innumerable factories and industrial plants in what had once been called the International Settlement.

Larry, carefully concealing himself in the cabin, looked out through the windshield at the forest of belching smokestacks. Shanghai was huge, callous, and aggressive, the natural magnet for people from every province of China, and even in the one-thousand-year-old quarter known as the Old City, nobody cared about the past. Shanghai, the nation's greatest seaport, lived completely in the present.

The barge finally reached the waterfront, where tall office buildings and handsome hotels — now used by the Red government as administration buildings — lined a broad avenue called the Bund. Once a gay, sparkling boulevard, the Bund had become drab and dull, its flashing neon signs replaced by government propaganda billboards, its fine shops closed.

Yang maneuvered his barge past forty or fifty mammoth freighters flying the flags of various Communist nations, and after painful, slow maneuvering finally moved to a wharf in an area dotted with many similar craft. Helped by David, he tied up at the dock, then turned off his dilapidated engine. The long voyage had come to an end.

Larry didn't know what to do next. Later tonight or perhaps in the morning longshoremen would unload Yang's cargo, and the bargeman, who hated the big city, planned to leave for home as soon as he could obtain food supplies and more drums of gasoline.

A single candle provided the only light in the cabin, and Larry shielded it with his hand as Yang and David returned to the cramped cell.

"I have business that takes me ashore," Yang said, then softened for the first time and grinned broadly as he extended his hand in a gesture of farewell. "Yang wishes you success," he told Larry, and rumpled David's hair. "If I abused you, young one, it was in a good cause."

Larry offered him several folded one-hundred-yuan notes. "Take these as a token of our appreciation," he said.

Yang drew himself erect and shook his head. "Every man who loves freedom must do what he can for it in his own way." He went to the door, paused momentarily, and added in an off-hand way, "If you wish, you may stay here for a time. It will be late when Yang returns, so he will not see you again." He vanished down the dark wharf.

"I'm certain Yang was telling us to wait," Larry said. "Li Yu-teh made careful plans for us, and he must have realized we'd be stranded here in Shanghai without help." Then he smiled, but took the precaution of removing the safety catch from his automatic.

They sat on the mats that had served as their beds for more than three weeks, and for the first time since their initial reunion at the school outside Peking had an opportunity to talk freely and at length. For the better part of two hours they filled each other in on the details of their lives during the years of their separation, and the candle was burning low when Larry suddenly interrupted his son's recital of how he had fared at the academy.

"Blow out the candle. I hear someone coming up the wharf!"

As David obeyed he saw the gleam of the automatic in his father's hand.

They waited tensely, and the footsteps drew nearer. Then the cabin door opened, and a bulky figure loomed in the frame. "Mr. Bliss?" the man asked, speaking English. Unable to see clearly in the gloom, he peered into the shack uncertainly.

194

Larry and David were better accustomed to the dark. The boy, responding to a silent command, sneaked behind the stranger and closed the door.

The man wheeled at the sound, and started to reach for a weapon.

"Raise your hands," Larry ordered, shoving the muzzle of the automatic into the stranger's back.

The man's hands shot high over his head.

"Search him, David."

The boy removed a pistol of Czechoslovakian make from the stranger's pocket and, backing away, pointed it at the man.

"Now light the candle again, son."

David struck a match with his free hand.

The interloper was tall and husky, but his narrow-lidded eyes and thin mouth gave him a lean appearance. He was dressed in a Western-style suit, complete with shirt, necktie, and breast-pocket handkerchief, the first such attire Larry had seen on anyone since arriving in China. "Who are you?" he asked coldly.

"My name is Ching Ke-yeh, and I wish you'd tell that boy to stop pointing my pistol at me. It's loaded and might go off."

Larry smiled, lowered his automatic, and gestured to his son. "Give Mr. Ching his weapon, David."

David obeyed, a trifle reluctantly.

Ching Ke-yeh pocketed the pistol, adjusted

195

his silk necktie, and smoothed his hair. "Are you ready to leave?" he asked. "We don't have too much time."

Larry remained cautious. "What plans do you have for us?"

"First I'll drive you to my house. I have some clean clothes waiting for you, and you'll no doubt want baths."

Larry and David laughed. After more than three weeks of trying to keep clean by washing in small basins of boiled Grand Canal water both yearned desperately for baths. "Thank you for your hospitality," Larry said. "But what then?"

Ching shrugged. "We'll have to play it by ear."

Larry raised an eyebrow.

"Didn't Yang tell you? I spent several years in the States. That's one of the reasons I speak good English. The regime is still looking hard for you — "

"And for the boy?"

"No, they're insisting he must be dead."

"I see." Larry evaluated his situation anew. "If I'm to have any mobility I'll need new identity papers. Mine are worthless. I'd be arrested instantly if I dared to show them."

"I have friends," Ching boasted, "but I'd better warn you in advance that forged credentials aren't cheap. But we'll talk about all that later."

196

Larry and David followed him, and both felt a pang of regret mixed with a vague trace of uneasiness as they stepped ashore from the primitive barge that had sheltered them for so long. A ten-year-old American-made automobile stood near the foot of the wharf, and as they headed toward it, Ching in the lead, Larry suddenly tensed. Three longshoremen in faded cotton tunics and trousers were lounging against pilings nearby, chatting idly as they rested.

The Shanghai weather was much milder than the bitter cold of Peking, and Larry realized he would call undue attention to himself if he turned up the collar of his coat and tried to conceal his face behind it. The mere fact that he was wearing the coat marked him as a personage of consequence.

But it was too late for him to take it off. The illumination in the immediate area was provided by a street light about twenty-five feet away, and he could only avert his face from its glare and hope that the longshoremen wouldn't recognize him as a Caucasian. When he was no more than a half-dozen paces from them, however, they became aware of the jaunty Ching Ke-yeh's approach. One of them muttered under his breath, and all three hurried back to the coal barge they had been unloading. Workers accused of laziness were sent off deep into the interior of China, usually without being granted the privilege of a hearing. There they were required to spend two to four years at hard labor, and these longshoremen wanted to take no chances.

Ching motioned David into the front seat, leaving the rear of the five-passenger car to Larry, who could either shift from side to side or sit in the middle of the seat in order to make himself inconspicuous, as the situation demanded.

Gears clashed and the car started off with a series of spine-jolting jerks. Whatever Ching's accomplishments, he was not an expert driver. But he was very pleased with himself and his possessions. "Not a bad car, huh? I could use a new one, though."

Larry guessed what he meant, but preferred that he spell it out. "I'm not an auto dealer."

Ching laughed far more loudly and heartily than the mild joke warranted. "Bliss, you have nerve, I'll admit that. But a fellow can't live on nerve. Agreed?"

Larry shrugged.

"Passage to Manila on a Polish freighter, with no questions asked, will take fifty thousand yuan — about twenty thousand American dollars."

"That's a great deal of money," Larry said.

"An Albanian ship that put in a few days ago is going on to Japan. It wouldn't cost as much, but the Albanians can't be trusted."

198

The Albanians, David thought, weren't the only ones.

"A man in your situation is prepared for emergencies, I'm sure," Ching continued.

"I do my best," Larry said.

"I doubt if many men in China carry as much as fifty thousand yuan with them." Ching glanced for an instant at his passenger.

"I don't know one," Larry replied pointedly.

"On the other hand, when a fellow is in a jam he can usually find friends to help bail him out."

Larry realized that he had to temporize. Ching's fee was outrageous, of course, but it was better to play for time than reject the demand too abruptly. "Most people have friends," he declared vaguely.

"You'll have to be on your way by tomorrow."

"You're very kind to look after us until then. What are you charging for refuge?"

Ching pretended to be insulted, but couldn't hide his lack of sincerity. "What do you think I am? I wouldn't take a penny for giving you a roof and something to eat." His tone hardened again. "Now, about those credentials. Eight thousand yuan for your new set of identity papers, and five thousand for the boy's."

"David doesn't need new papers." Larry saw no reason to explain that his son already carried a set of false credentials.

199

"Oh?" Ching transferred his attention from the traffic to David for a moment, his eyes bright and hard. "In that case it'll cost you ten thousand for yours."

There could be no doubt that the man was a greedy extortionist, but Larry felt he had no choice. "If I must," he said.

"In advance," Ching told him.

"I'll give you five thousand in advance, and the rest when you deliver the papers," Larry said flatly.

Ching turned a corner at high speed, savagely, the tires protesting. "Who are you to set conditions?"

"Someone who doesn't intend to be cheated," Larry said.

There was no further conversation as they drove into the district that had been called the French concession prior to the Reds' rise to power. Two- and three-story private houses, most of them handsome and substantial, lined well-lighted, broad avenues. Lawns were neatly tended, and if it hadn't been for the lacquer and Oriental cherry trees, the graceful camphorwoods and dwarf pines, the section would have resembled a prosperous suburb of a city in the United States.

"I've got a great house," Ching said, his good humor returning as he swung into the gravel driveway of an imposing brick dwelling. "It belonged to an American bank manager, but the government gave it to me when he was thrown out of the country. You should have kept yourself in good with the fellows at the top, Bliss. Life here can be a terrific racket." He led the way to the second floor of the house.

Larry and David found themselves outside the door of a large tiled bathroom.

"I sent my wife out for the evening," Ching told them, glancing at a gold wristwatch. "You have exactly an hour to get cleaned up and eat some food before you bed down for the night in the attic. In fact I'll bring your food up to you there, just in case she returns a little early. I don't want her to know I've got a couple of fugitives in the place. Anything special you'd like to eat?" His manner now was that of a jovial host.

David shook his head.

"Whatever you have at hand will be delicious, I'm sure." Larry paused for an instant. "I must confess that ever since I was forced to go into hiding I've been dreaming of eating some young litchi nuts. I'd be grateful if you have a few."

Ching was amused. "False hunger, they call it in the prison camps — and you haven't even been arrested yet! It would take too long to boil them, you know."

"I'll gladly take them raw," Larry replied. "Later, somewhere, I can either roast or boil them myself."

Ching shrugged. "Okay, if that's all it takes to make you happy." He disappeared down the carpeted stairs.

David looked at his father curiously, sure that he had some ulterior motive. The request seemed very odd.

Larry offered no explanation. "Climb into the shower, David, and I'll keep watch. Then I'll want you to do the same for me. Let me know if he drives off somewhere or if other cars show up here. I'm sure Ching isn't a member of Li Yu-teh's underground organization. He's just a money-grubbing opportunist, so we've got to be very, very careful."

A quarter of an hour later, after both had showered and Larry had shaved with a razor he found in the bathroom cabinet, Ching reappeared with clean tunics and trousers, underclothes, and socks that fitted reasonably well.

By the time they were dressed he came up the stairs again, carrying a heavily laden tray, and led them to a small door opening onto a ladder to the attic above. "How's this for service?" he asked. "I've even got your litchi nuts, Bliss." Once again his manner underwent a swift transformation. "Now a word on business. Stay in the attic until I come for you tomorrow, and don't make any noise. I don't want my wife alarmed. All right? Hand over the ten thousand, and I'll have your new identity papers by morning."

Larry carefully counted out half the amount that the man had requested. "You'll get five thousand more when you deliver the credentials, Ching," he said, his manner unyielding.

An expression of anger appeared in the man's eyes for a moment, but he pocketed the money without comment and turned away.

Larry sent David ahead to the attic, handed the tray up to him, and followed after closing the door. "Ah, there are windows overlooking both the front and back of the house. Good. You watch at that side, and I'll take this." He moved to his self-appointed post, carrying the tray. "We've just spent five thousand yuan for papers we'll never see, but it couldn't be helped. He'd have screamed himself silly if we'd refused to give him any money. Let's just say we've paid five thousand for some clean clothes and a meal."

David, stationing himself at the other window, was surprised to see his father remove the lid of a steaming teapot, sniff the contents, and then, dipping a finger into the liquid, put an experimental drop on his tongue.

"Just as I thought," Larry said. "Friend

Ching is too clever for his own good — or ours. This tea has been doped with crude opium — laudanum, it's called. He wants to put us to sleep and then call in the Security Service. I'm willing to bet on it."

David was even more astonished when he saw his father remove his tunic and shirt, then start to peel away the semi-hard shells of the green litchi nuts with a paring knife.

"Keep watch, David. Don't look at me."

The boy turned reluctantly and stared out of the attic window into the street. After a wait of only a few minutes he called softly. "There's a car turning into the driveway."

Larry snapped off the overhead light and joined his son, hastily stuffing his shirt into his trousers again and buttoning his tunic. Another old American automobile stopped in the driveway, and a moment later a woman emerged. She was wearing her hair in a Western style, and was dressed in a silk *cheongsam*.

"Mrs. Ching shares her husband's expensive tastes," Larry said in a low voice. "Birds of a feather."

David turned — and gasped. His father's skin was now a dull, copper-like brown, and even the pupils of his eyes were dark. He would be accepted anywhere as an Oriental.

Larry smiled. "The juice of young litchi nuts is a very effective stain. I'd have done this long ago, but the young unripened nuts aren't available in Peking or anywhere else in the north at this time of year. They're sold only in the south during the winter and early spring. I was relying on Ching's fancy tastes. He's the type who'd have delicacies in his larder."

David continued to stare at him. "But your eyes are different too."

"I've put on contact lenses that were made for just this emergency. Now it's time to leave, son. This house is a little too crowded for my taste. Walk on the balls of your feet, and don't make a sound."

They crept down the ladder, and Larry cautiously raised the latch of the attic door, which he closed after them. Then they headed down the corridor toward the back staircase, hugging the wall, and Larry lifted a warning hand when they heard muffled voices in a bedroom off to their right.

They hesitated for a moment, but the voices continued, and Larry started down the back staircase, David close behind him.

His plan of action was simple but direct. They would leave by way of the garage, which opened onto the kitchen, as he had noted when they had first arrived, and would steal one of the cars in the driveway. The sound of a running engine might alert Ching, but they had to take the chance. In any event, the man would soon discover that his intended victims had vanished.

It wouldn't be difficult for the authorities to trace an automobile thief in a city where cars were scarce, but the need for rapid transportation was urgent. Larry estimated that the house stood about three miles from the Shanghai business district, where the railroad stations were located, and four from the waterfront, where it might be possible to bribe the owner of a launch or junk. Waiting for a bus would be a waste of precious time, the risk of hailing a taxicab — assuming he could even find one — would be too great, so he had no alternative. Only by taking one of Ching's cars could he hope to leave Shanghai before he and David were apprehended.

The kitchen was empty and dark. David inadvertently brought down a foot too sharply on the tiled floor, and Larry halted as his son clapped a hand over his mouth. The sound seemed to reverberate through the house, but after a moment or two Larry breathed more easily. He smiled at his son to indicate that no harm had been done, and they started again, moving very slowly and carefully toward the door that opened onto the garage.

The two-car garage was as thoroughly American in design as the rest of the house. The double doors were open, indicating that

Ching probably intended to put his cars away for the night after the Security Service picked up his drugged "guests." A half-moon cast its light across a portion of the cement floor, and the beam was reflected in a stack of three-gallon gasoline cans stacked in one corner.

Each of them bore a legend indicating that it was the property of the Red Chinese army, and Larry smiled cynically. In spite of the gasoline shortage that plagued the country, it appeared that Ching was able to beg or borrow, steal or commandeer what he needed.

Suddenly a man stepped out of the shadows in the far corner of the garage. "Going somewhere?" Ching asked.

Larry found himself looking into the muzzle of an ugly snub-nosed revolver.

12

LARRY QUICKLY TOOK STOCK of the situation. Evidently Ching Ke-yeh had heard or seen his intended victims in the second-floor corridor and had beaten them to the garage by racing down the front stairs. Such details were not important however. What mattered was that he was here, armed with a weapon that he was obviously ready to use.

"Stretch!" Ching commanded.

There was no choice, and Larry slowly raised his hands above his head.

Meanwhile David's mind was working furiously too. Ching seemed to be paying no attention to him, so he sidled off into the shadows beyond the moonlight, hoping to creep up on the man from the rear. He moved two steps closer, then two more.

But Ching appeared to have eyes in the back of his head. Continuing to train his revolver on Larry, he half turned, and his free hand shot out, catching David full in the face. Completely surprised by the sudden blow, the boy was slammed against the garage wall. He slumped to the cement floor in a daze.

The momentary diversion was all Larry needed. He aimed a sharp kick at the hand that held the revolver, much like a punter letting fly at a football.

Ching emitted a howl of pain as the pistol soared from his hand, landed somewhere in the shadows, and skidded out of sight. The odds had been equalized, and Larry threw himself forward. They grappled, each man trying in vain to land a solid punch, crashed to the cement floor, and rolled over and over. Larry had no opportunity to draw his own automatic. The second or two he would have needed to reach into his pocket for it would have given Ching just enough time to gain the advantage.

The American landed two blows, one to the face and the other to the body, but they did not carry enough force to incapacitate Ching.

Neither man was able to regain his feet, and the slugging match continued as each freed an arm for an instant at a time, just long enough to lash out, before being pinned down again. Larry soon realized that he would have to win quickly: Ching was several years younger and was brawnier.

He redoubled his efforts, calling on his reserves of strength. But Ching slipped out of his grasp just long enough to slam Larry's head onto the concrete floor. Before Larry quite knew what was happening he was flat on his back, with Ching's strong fingers closing around his throat.

Larry's legs thrashed, and he tried in vain to pry away the thick fingers that were slowly squeezing the air from his lungs. He blacked out for a moment, and as he regained full consciousness he realized that he was weakening rapidly.

David, who was slumped against the far wall, shook his head repeatedly to clear it. At last he was able to focus again and was horrified when he saw his father being overpowered. The boy staggered to his feet and frenziedly began to search for the pistol that had been knocked from Ching's hand.

Precious seconds passed as he searched for it without success. He decided to jump on Ching's back in order to haul the man off.

Larry saw his son with bleary eyes, and knew that the boy was too slight, that he lacked the weight and strength to distract Ching. Only one hope remained.

"David," he gasped. "My boot!" He kicked hard on the floor.

Completely bewildered, David stood still. Then he saw something black emerge from the heel of his father's boot, caught a glimpse of metal beyond it, and realized that he was staring at a knife. He bent down, grasped the hilt, and pulled out the double-edged blade.

David steadied himself, took a deep breath, and using all his strength plunged the blade into Ching's back.

For an instant the man remained motionless; then he slumped and toppled to one side.

David was numb.

Larry loosened the fingers that still held his throat and freed himself. Slowly, groggily he hauled himself to his feet and sucked air into his lungs. Gradually the garage stopped spinning.

"Thanks," he said hoarsely, and took command. A single glance was enough to assure him that Ching was dead. He bent down, removed the knife, and after wiping the blade on the man's clothes slipped it back into the hiding place in his boot. Then he made a swift search of the dead man's pockets.

The first prize he found was a set of car keys. The second, enclosed in a leather wallet, was an even greater prize, and he smiled grimly as he flipped through Ching's official indentification papers.

He dropped the wallet and keys into his own pocket, stood, and dragged the man's body to the far side of the garage, leaving it behind the pile of gasoline cans. As he turned away he saw Ching's revolver, and picked it up. "Your practice in marksmanship at the academy may come in handy before we're out of this jam," he said to David. "I'll carry this for now though." He went out to Ching's car, in the driveway.

David followed and climbed in beside his father. The engine started; they backed out into the street and headed toward the Shanghai business district.

"At best," Larry said, "we'll have a breathing spell of a few hours. Mrs. Ching undoubtedly heard the car start, and I hope she thought her husband was driving somewhere. But we can't count on that. She may investigate and find her husband's body. If she does, she'll notify the Security Service."

Larry lapsed into silence, concentrating on the heavier traffic as they approached the center of the city. There were far more cars in Shanghai than in Peking, principally because the executives of the many industrial plants were permitted the luxury of owning automobiles. Pedicabs were everywhere too, and pedestrians dodged in and out of traffic, often walking in the streets rather than confining themselves to the sidewalks.

David realized that they were driving toward the waterfront and assumed that his father hoped to arrange an escape by ship before the authorities were alerted.

Larry reached the Bund, the great boulevard facing the harbor, and drove down it slowly. Suddenly he laughed in quiet triumph. "There's the old King George Hotel," he said. "It's still used as a hotel — for visitors from foreign countries. I was relying on this. Look at all the cars in the parking lot!"

David asked no questions as his father drove into the lot.

"Every policeman in Shanghai will be searching for this car by morning," Larry continued. "This is one of the last places they'll think of hunting for it. With luck, it might even sit here for a day or two before they come across it." He parked, turned off the engine, and put the keys into the glove compartment. "Now we'll stretch our legs. Walk quickly, but make it appear as though we're strolling."

David was surprised when his father started back toward the business district instead of crossing the Bund to the waterfront.

Larry took care to address his son in Mandarin now. Even though he spoke very softly, he didn't want some casual passerby jolted by hearing a snatch of a foreign language. "If the car should be found," he said, "they'll think we're trying to leave the country by sea. We can't, actually. By now the reward for our cap-

213

ture is probably far greater than any ship's owner or captain could earn by giving us passage. But it's what I want the Security Service to believe."

Once more he fell silent, and didn't speak again until he motioned his son toward one of the many shops that stayed open through the evening. "Do you speak the Shanghai dialect?"

"Only Mandarin and Hopeh."

"Then don't say anything in here." Larry led him into the shop and bought two small inexpensive suitcases of canvas.

They resumed their walk, making several more stops for purchases, which included spare shirts and underclothes, toilet articles, and other odds and ends needed by travelers. Larry handled these transactions smoothly, addressing the shopkeepers in the local tongue, which was a rather bewildering mixture of the country's principal dialects.

After going eight or ten blocks they came to a huge barnlike building of stone, wood, and glass, grimy with the dirt of a great city. Carved in stone over the main entrance was the name "Hu-Hang-Jung," and David knew where they were. He had read about the Hu-Hang-Jung at the academy, and now understood his father's strategy. They had come to the southern railway station, the Shanghai-Hangchow-Ningpo, and the boy realized that they would try to escape by train.

They went into the station and walked straight to a ticket counter. There Larry took his first great gamble, presenting Ching's credentials as his own and hoping that the clerk wouldn't study him too closely to see if his features matched the photograph of Ching Ke-yeh. He passed muster, and after paying the clerk the expected bribe, as he had done in Tientsin, they walked away from the counter with two tickets and sleeping-car reservations on the midnight coastal train to Foochow, the once-great tea-export center to the south. There, the following day, they would change to a train on the new roadbed that stretched toward the great metropolis of the south: Canton.

David needed no further explanations from his father. Across the border from Canton lay the British crown colony of Hong Kong — and freedom.

Thirty minutes remained before the train's scheduled departure, and Larry used the time to good advantage. He bought several loaves of millet bread and rolls of sausage meat, which he wrapped in newspapers and packed in his suitcase. A vendor at the far side of the station was selling rice cakes, so he purchased an ample supply, which he handed to David. Finally he bought three flasks of barley water, having discovered on his ride from Tientsin

215

to Peking that the tap water on trains in China was intended only for washing, not drinking.

David marveled at his father's foresight. They would be able to eat in their room on the train, and would be spared the necessity — and risk — of going into the public dining car.

A few passengers were starting toward the track where the train for Foochow was standing, but Larry deliberately loitered in the station until the crowds heading for the train grew thicker. Then he nodded, and they sauntered toward it, acting like two carefree travelers who didn't have a worry in the world.

Suddenly David's step faltered. Two members of the Security Service, revolvers in holsters hanging from their belts, were standing beside the entrance to the track, studying the passengers who streamed past them.

Larry reacted promptly. He touched his son's arm in a swift, reassuring gesture, and casually pulled his hat lower over the back of his head to make certain that his hair, far lighter than that of any Chinese, would not show at the nape of his neck and betray him. Then, his calm monumental, he halted only an arm's length from the two guards to buy a twisted paper cone of roasted watermelon seeds from a vendor.

Either his disguise was excellent or his

216

boldness paid dividends; whatever the reason, the Security Service men paid no attention to him after glancing once in his direction.

Larry offered the roasted seeds to his son as they moved on down the platform. David was afraid he would choke, and shook his head. "Eat some," his father told him in a fierce whisper.

David obeyed, knowing that a refusal would immediately draw attention to him. No Chinese boy in his right mind ever rejected a delicacy like watermelon seeds.

When they reached their sleeping car other passengers stood in line waiting to board it, all of them wearing expensively tailored tunics and carrying bulging briefcases. These men were the elite of Red China: plant managers, government officials, and high-ranking members of the Communist party who were accustomed to rapid service and deferential treatment. The harassed car attendant, who was required by law to check the identity papers of everyone in his car, looked through the credentials in a perfunctory manner. Obviously he was afraid of antagonizing important men.

David tensed as the man leafed through his own false papers, and did the same with Ching's credentials, which his father was carrying. Then the compartment door closed. Larry locked it, pulled down the bamboo blind that

217

shaded the window, and smiled at his son. That smile — and all it signified — was enough for David. He felt warm and secure again, and when the train pulled slowly out of the Shanghai station the evening's nightmare faded from his mind.

The train stopped twice during the night, first at the bustling city of Hangchow, then at the smaller port of Ningpo. From there it cut through the delta farmlands of Chekiang Province, where hard-working peasants labored ceaselessly to earn a living from soil exhausted by their ancestors. Larry and David ate a breakfast of millet bread and sausage washed down with barley water and did not venture from their compartment.

David had something on his mind, and after several false starts he blurted, "I want to talk to you about something."

"Of course."

"When you first came to see me at the academy and told me who you were, I — well, I mostly didn't believe you. But even the part of me that did wasn't very happy about it. I had a crazy idea that you didn't care about me — "

"I know, son. You'd been through a rough time."

David gestured impatiently. "Let me finish. For a long time I wished you were dead. Like

218

Mom. I pretended I didn't have any parents. That way I could get along." He was finding it very hard to express himself.

Larry wanted to help, but realized that David had to speak his mind alone.

"I know I'm not the only reason you came to China. And at first I tried to tell myself that I was just incidental. But I've learned the sort of person you are. I think you're the greatest father a boy ever had."

"Let's finish this sausage," Larry said huskily.

David nodded. "Okay. I'm hungrier than I thought, Dad." It was the first time he had addressed Larry as "Dad" since they had been together.

In midmorning the train crossed into Fukien Province. Off to the west towered the lofty peaks of the mountain range that sealed off Fukien, making it the most remote and inaccessible of all China's seacoast provinces. The weather was becoming noticeably warmer, and although it was still winter in Peking the air here was balmy and soft. David opened the window, sat back in his seat, and allowed himself the long-forbidden luxury of daydreaming about home. In Vermont the basketball season was ending, boys were taking baseball and gloves and bats from attics, and the fish were beginning to run. Soon, perhaps, he would be there.

Larry had not asked the attendant to disconnect the loudspeaker in the compartment, and suddenly the metallic, impersonal voice of a newscaster interrupted David's idle thoughts. "The comrade commissar of Shanghai police," the man said in somber tones, "regrets to announce the foul murder of Ching Ke-yeh, assistant deputy secretary of the Shanghai Communist party. Comrades everywhere will mourn his death. But they may take comfort. The police are preparing to arrest the robber-assassins who took the life of this loyal and devoted servant of the people."

The sound of band music floated through the speaker again. Even though the air was warm, David shivered.

Larry pondered for a time. "We can't judge much from that broadcast," he said at last. "I can't really tell what the police know."

David's voice trembled. "He said they're going to announce our arrest."

"Maybe, son. Maybe not. All I know is that they haven't revealed all the information they've gathered. They didn't mention the stolen car, you'll note."

"Maybe they've found it by now in that hotel parking lot, Dad."

"Perhaps. On the other hand they may be keeping quiet in order to catch us off guard." Larry coolly inspected his automatic and then checked the revolver he was carrying for David. "I hope you'll never need to use this. If everything continues to go smoothly we'll be across the border in another twenty-four to thirty-six hours." He looked at his watch, then reached for the food.

Excitement ruined David's appetite, but his father insisted that he eat, and between them they finished their supplies. Rain began to fall, making it necessary for them to close the window, and the heat in the compartment became stifling. They suffered without complaint, and David, in spite of his discomfort, was soothed by the steady beat of raindrops on the windowpane.

It was still drizzling when late in the afternoon the train crawled into the station at Foochow, the capital of Fukien Province. The attendant went through the sleeping car to make certain that all the passengers left, and David, carrying his own canvas bag, walked out onto the damp wind-swept platform with his father. His heart sank when he saw two squads of armed soldiers standing at the entrance to the station itself. A rope cordon had been erected, and the passengers were required to pass in single file, pausing to present their identity papers to a slender, dapper man in an oilskin raincoat and hat who sat at a table that had been set up just outside the entrance.

Larry made sure that his hat was firmly in place at the back of his head. "Don't lose your nerve, David," he murmured, and went forward boldly.

David saw that his father was carrying Ching's credentials in his left hand, and that his right was plunged into the pocket of his tunic. The boy knew that he was holding his automatic, ready to use it at once if trouble developed.

They stood patiently in the long line of passengers, moving forward inch by inch. Their situation was doubly complicated now, and both knew it. Larry was carrying the credentials of a man whose murder had been publicly announced, and if the inspector recognized the name of Ching Ke-yeh there would be immediate fireworks.

Several of the more important officials among the passengers placed one-hundred-yuan notes in their identity papers, and the man at the desk proved himself adept at removing the money while flicking through the papers, which he returned to their owners after no more than a token examination.

David saw his father follow the example of the other men, and at last his turn came. He and the inspector exchanged a few words, and David froze. They were speaking a tongue that was completely alien to him. All at once he remembered something he had been taught at the academy: the dialect of Fukien was unique and bore virtually no resemblance to Mandarin or the languages of other provinces.

Larry was passed quickly, his one-hundred-yuan note making the man behind the desk pliably friendly. Then it was David's turn, and the boy saw that his father had drifted on through the station entrance, pretending they weren't traveling together. David was momentarily stunned by the knowledge that for the moment he was on his own.

The inspector went through the false papers that had been prepared in Peking by Li Yu-the, and David hoped he looked unconcerned. Then the man said something to him — in the dialect of Fukien.

The boy was tempted to reply in Mandarin, but remembered Li Chuh's warning. The authorities were looking for a runaway from the renowned Sun Yat-sen Academy whom they had, for their own purposes, reported as "dead," and who spoke the purest of Chinese tongues. So, taking a deep breath, he replied in the broadest and crudest Hopeh that he could devise. "I don't understand the honored comrade's words," he said.

The inspector looked him up and down. "Where are you going?" The man spoke Mandarin now.

David, still avoiding the dialect of the educated classes, replied in Hopeh. "To the home of my uncle in Canton."

"For what purpose?"

"I don't know, honored comrade. My father died, and I shall live with my uncle." David was improvising glibly, and a sudden flash of inspiration impelled him to add, "In another two years, when I'm old enough, I'm going to be a soldier." He looked with simulated admiration at the bayonet-bearing, steel-helmeted troops.

His play-acting proved to be unexpectedly effective. The official called something to the soldiers in the Fukien dialect, and all of them laughed coarsely. Then, to the boy's relief, the inspector handed him his credentials, together with a slip of paper bearing the legend, "Permit for Bearer to Board Canton Express."

David moved on into the station. His father had sauntered ahead to buy several newspapers, and then wandered toward a bulletin board where photographs of China's atomic-bomb explosions were being exhibited. David joined him there.

"Buy some food for the next stage of our journey," Larry said in an undertone, "and meet me on the Canton Express platform in ten minutes. It's better that we separate. There are guards everywhere, and they may see through my disguise. Be sure you're prompt. Our train was late, and the Canton Express leaves in exactly twelve minutes." Giving his son no chance to reply, he left the station and disappeared.

David obeyed orders and purchased a stack of meat-and-rice cakes, several flasks of barley water, and a string of dried smoked fish from vendors in the station. Then with three minutes to spare, he went to the platform where the Canton Express was waiting. He handed his permit to the two guards stationed there and was admitted to the platform.

There he loitered, watching the entrance and, beyond it, the large clock on the station wall. The minute hand moved, and after an agony of suspense moved again. Nine minutes had passed, and there was no sign of his father.

Another minute dragged by. The train would leave in a hundred and twenty seconds. David decided that, no matter what happened, he wouldn't board it alone.

Larry came through the gate calmly, handing his permit to the guards with a flourish and strolling as though he had all the time in the world.

But David knew instantly, from the lines

around his father's mouth, that something had gone wrong.

They went together to their sleeping car, and the attendant there shuffled through their credentials quickly in order to complete the chore before the train started.

Not until they were alone in their compartment did Larry speak. "I went into Foochow to make a few purchases," he said, "and had some bad luck. I'll tell you about it shortly."

David watched him unwrap a package. In it were some half-ripe litchi nuts, and Larry used them to deepen the stain on his face, neck, and hands. Then he opened a small jar, shook some powder onto his head, and began to rub his scalp vigorously.

David was astonished to see his father's hair turning darker.

"I went into an apothecary shop for some black antimony," Larry explained. "Women have used it for thousands of years — for cosmetic purposes. It's too risky to keep my hat on at all times, and this stuff will make my hair look black until I wash it out." He turned to wash his hands in the basin at the far side of the compartment. "It was in the apothecary shop that I had my bad luck, and I waited there as long as I dared before meeting you. I — "

A tap at the door caused him to break off

sharply, and he reached for the automatic in his pocket without drying his hands. "One moment!" he called in Mandarin, and indicated with a gesture that he wanted David to stand aside.

The boy did as he was bidden, gripping his own revolver.

Larry unbolted the door and opened it slowly.

A blond woman stood in the entrance, and David was astonished to see Laura Zandulsky.

"May I come in?" she asked in Mandarin.

Larry shrugged, his right hand still in his tunic pocket.

Laura closed the door. "Well," she said, switching to English, "you're traveling with your ward. Hello, David."

The boy nodded to her, but did not speak.

"Your disguise is excellent, Richie," she continued, "but I'd know you anywhere. I recognized you instantly in the apothecary shop."

David knew now what had delayed his father.

"You've been a very busy man, Richie. I gather you were particularly active in Shanghai."

Larry said nothing. "I don't have much time to talk. A couple of Security Service men are escorting me. They've been with me all the way from Peking, in fact. They're in the dining car right now. I excused myself to wash my hands before dinner."

David was aware of his father's tension, and thought how difficult it must be to play several roles concurrently. Suddenly, without warning, Richard L. Bliss had been forced to reappear on the scene.

"I'm sorry you're having trouble," Larry said.

The woman's temper flared. "You knew Ho F'ang would be after me as soon as he suspected you of selling information to the Russians. He interrogated me for several days, and I might have broken down and admitted that we were working together if the Polish embassy hadn't intervened."

"I see." Larry continued to say as little as possible.

"When Ho F'ang took you into custody I was badly frightened, but I'm grateful to you for keeping your mouth shut about our operations. I might have spent the rest of my life in prison instead of being thrown out of the country. I just hope you realize I want nothing more to do with you. If we should be seen together, and they find out you're Richie Bliss, I'll be in trouble all over again. That's why I've come here — to beg you to leave me alone."

Larry was relieved. She was still afraid that

Bliss might reveal to the authorities that she had been working for the Russians. He decided to press his advantage. "How do I know you aren't following me so that you can report me to the Security Service? You might have made some kind of arrangement with Ho F'ang."

There was a note of savage desperation in Laura's voice now. "I promise you all I want is to get out of this country. I'd have flown home to Warsaw straight from Peking, but Polish planes aren't being allowed to land there these days. So our consul-general in Canton is providing me with a car at noon tomorrow. I'm to deliver it to one of our people in Hong Kong, and I'll fly from there. You — you won't cross me up, Richie?"

"I can't without implicating myself."

Laura sighed. "Who would have thought it would all end like this? You're a fugitive, and I'm walking a tightrope." She held out her hand. "Good-bye, David. Good luck, Richie."

The door closed, and she was gone.

There was a silence. "I wish I knew what that was all about," David said at last.

"It's both good and bad," his father told him. "What I don't like is that there are Security Service agents on board this train. We can't afford to make any mistakes."

"Will that woman give us away to them?"

"No, I'm sure she was telling the truth. Not

that she wouldn't turn me over to them if it would do her any good, but she'd be in more trouble herself. You see, son, she and Bliss were spying for Russia. Bliss was conveniently murdered while he was on a trip out of the country — because they didn't have enough evidence against him to hang him. Then Ho F'ang tried to get information from Laura Zandulsky, but the Poles are obligated to protect her, and they're anxious to get her out of China."

Again there was a silence, and David looked curiously at his father. "You're smiling, Dad."

"I guess I am. Richard L. Bliss did us a favor, David."

"I don't understand."

"Our only hope of leaving China is to cross the Hong Kong border. We and Laura are headed in the same direction."

The boy's eyes widened. "But she said she's being followed by the Security Service."

"I know. That's one of the unfortunate complications. So we'll just have to keep on as we've been doing — improvise and take one step at a time."

"Then — how did Bliss do us a favor?"

"He sealed Laura's mouth. As long as she still believes me to be Bliss she can't lift a finger to hurt me. And she can be helpful to us — in spite of herself."

13

LARRY AND DAVID kept watch through the long night and the following morning, taking turns sleeping and eating. The weather became increasingly hot and humid as the train moved south, and by midmorning the travelers found themselves in the tropics. Larry opened the compartment window, and when David was not on duty watching the door he gazed out at sun-baked, tortured fields. Land was so precious in overcrowded China that not one acre was allowed to lie fallow. Women and children carried buckets of water, balancing one at each end of a long bamboo pole, and men fed the parched earth to encourage the growth of food so desperately needed in southern China.

Here and there the boy saw an old tractor, but most of the peasants still used methods thousands of years old. Too poor to own machines, much less oxen or horses, even those

231

working on state-owned farms harnessed themselves to plows and wearily trudged back and forth across the fields.

The train made a brief stop at the little town of Tsengshinhsien, less than an hour's journey from Canton. Vendors swarmed down the platform selling water ices and cool drinks to the passengers. Those in the sleeping cars leaned out of their compartment windows to make their purchases, and the windows of the barnlike coaches were even more crowded.

Larry debated briefly with himself whether to lower the bamboo blinds and thus avoid taking the chance of unnecessary exposure to Security Service agents. But he decided that he and David would be even more conspicuous if they withdrew completely. The heat was so intense that anyone who failed to make a purchase would attract attention.

David bought two small chilled watermelons while his father continued to keep watch at the door. As he was paying for the fruit and waiting to be given his change the boy saw another vendor approaching, and something in the man's attitude struck him as odd. For a moment it was difficult to determine what seemed out of place, but suddenly David realized what was wrong. The wineskin slung over the man's shoulder was new, as was his hat, and, unlike the other peddlers, he was wearing shoes.

"Dad!"

"What's wrong?"

"I don't like the looks of a man out here."

"Take my place at the door." Larry moved swiftly to the window, then said in a low voice, "Drop to the floor, David. I don't want him to see you."

The vendor, a tall man with discolored teeth, was pausing at the window of each compartment and trying to peer inside. Equally suspicious was his lack of interest in disposing of his wares. The others ranging up and down the hot, dusty platform were shouting at the tops of their hoarse voices, but he said nothing as he concentrated on his search.

Larry felt reasonably safe for the moment, and made up his mind to meet boldness with boldness. The litchi-nut stain and black antimony made him look thoroughly Chinese, and he knew he could pass muster as a government official or plant manager. He had never seen the man, and concluded that the agent — if the vendor was intended an agent — wouldn't know him on sight, either. So he stood at the open window, blocking the view of David with his body.

The vendor stopped at the adjoining window, then came closer.

Larry elected to address him in the unusual Fukien dialect. "I want no wine, thank you," he said politely.

The man obviously failed to understand him and didn't seem to care.

Larry shook his head to emphasize his words.

The vendor moved on, his eyes blank.

A few moments later the train started off on the last leg of the journey to Canton.

David cut open the watermelons and began to eat.

Larry smiled, but there was no humor in his eyes. "I wonder if you can remember our deer-stalking trips when you were younger."

"Sure, Dad!"

"Then you may recall a theory of mine, that the hunted has a natural advantage over the hunter because he's protected by his instinct for self-preservation. We'll soon find out whether that theory is right."

The train slowed to a crawl as it passed through the teeming jungle of flimsy shacks and substantial houses, crowded slums and new apartment buildings of Canton. Sophisticated, vulgar, and independent, this great metropolitan center of more than two million people, located on the delta of the Pearl River, had long been a thorn in the side of China's new government.

Her citizens, many of them thrifty, shrewd, and highly intelligent, had migrated to every part of the world by the tens of thousands, carrying with them an image that the people of other lands had come to regard as typical of China. In North and South America, Europe and Africa and Australia, the slender, industrious Cantonese had prospered as shopkeepers and merchants, bankers and professional men.

Those who had remained at home were tough and resilient too, stubbornly rejecting the attempts of the Red regime to cast them into the mold that people in other parts of China had accepted. David looked out of the compartment window and was able to understand why there had been such envy and frustration in the voices of his teachers at the academy when they had spoken of Canton.

Relatively few drab uniforms of tunics and trousers were worn by either sex. The women of Canton were dressed in colorful *cheongsams*, the men in lightweight suits and short-sleeved, Western-style shirts. In a vacant lot near the railroad tracks a group of boys was playing baseball, the game having gained popularity in the city by way of Japan, where it had become as much of an institution as it was in the United States.

The pitcher uncoiled and threw, and the batter lunged hard at the ball, but missed.

"Fooled him," David said. "From here it looked like a curve."

Larry hated to interrupt him, but had no choice. "Here, son. Take your pistol."

David returned to reality with a jolt.

"Leave everything else. We're traveling light from now on."

David dropped his weapon into his tunic pocket, and was surprised to see his father lower the compartment window as far as he could.

The train was snaking through the railroad yards now at a speed of no more than five miles per hour as it headed toward the domed North Station a few hundred yards away.

"Climb onto the sill with me," Larry said. "That's it. We're going to disappoint Ho F'ang's reception committee. All right, son. Ready? Jump!"

They leaped to the ground together, landing on hands and knees on the cinder roadbed.

"On your feet, David!" Larry commanded.

For the benefit of passengers aboard the Canton Express who might be glancing in their direction, they tried to look casually natural as they made their way across the many tracks that crisscrossed the vast yards.

David picked bits of cinder out of the palms of his hands.

"Do you see those sheds directly ahead? That's where we're going. Beyond them is a street the Reds call Karl Marx Avenue. I imagine that the high fence on the far side of the sheds is electrified, but there must be a gate somewhere. We'll soon find out."

Before they could walk more than a few paces two railroad guards suddenly appeared from behind the rear coach of an empty train standing in the yards. Both were carrying rifles, which they promptly unlimbered.

"You, there!" one of them called in the fluid Cantonese dialect. "Halt!"

"Make a dash for the empty train," Larry directed. "Crouch low."

Almost doubled over, David raced at top speed beside his father. He remembered from his military training at the academy that most riflemen had a tendency to fire too high.

A rifle cracked, and a high-pitched whine sounded directly overhead. Then there was a second shot, and a third. For the first time in his life David was the target of live ammunition.

Larry leaped onto the platform of a car on the empty train and, in almost the same motion, hauled his son up beside him.

The old wood of the coach trim was splintered by a bullet only inches from David's face.

Larry pulled the boy into the dusty coach. "Don't show yourself above window level, son. They'll expect us to go out on the other side toward the fence. Instead we'll make our way down the length of this train."

Still crouching, they continued to run. The sound of rifle fire had stopped, and after passing through four cars Larry halted and peered through a dirt-smudged window. "Ah, that's more like it. They're looking for us about a hundred and fifty yards to our rear." He gave the boy a brief respite to regain his breath. "Our immediate goal is that supply shed. You'll have to cover twenty yards of open space, but I want you to run as you've never done before. If they see us before we reach it we're lost."

David took a deep breath. "I can do it."

"All right. You first. Go!"

David braced himself, made a wild leap, and dashed toward the dilapidated shed. Just as he reached it one of the railroad guards turned, and the boy flattened himself against the wall of the building, not daring to move.

The guard raised a hand to shade his eyes from the bright sun, said something to his companion, and turned away again.

At the same instant Larry jumped from the platform and sped toward his son. "Get inside!" he ordered.

The door of the shed was open, and David slipped through it.

Larry coolly studied the high fence of steel

mesh before joining him. On the far side stood the relative refuge of Karl Marx Avenue, which was strangely deserted, and in the distance they could hear the blare of trumpets and crash of cymbals.

It appeared that the shed was used by the railroad guards as a dumping ground for trash. Larry poked around in the refuse, shoving aside bits of stale food, and seemed to be looking for something. David didn't dare interrupt him, knowing that the two guards who had fired at them were undoubtedly giving an alarm and that the entire area would soon be alive with armed men.

"Here we are!" Larry exclaimed, and picked up an empty beer can, which he then proceeded to flatten under his heel. "Trust the Cantonese to insist on using cans, even though there's a shortage of metal in China. How good are you at climbing?"

"Okay, I guess."

"You'll have to be better than that, son. Stand ready, and I'll give you a boost. You'll be able to get a toe hold in the mesh. Go straight to the top, and then jump to the ground on the other side. It's only about ten feet. Whatever you do, don't climb down."

David nodded, asking no questions.

His father went cautiously into the open again, shoved the flattened can toward the fence, and then prodded it closer with a stick. "Out here beside me!" he called softly. "That's it. Get ready!"

There was a flash of blue flame as the metal can made contact with the fence. Larry immediately caught hold of David, and, using all his strength, lifted the boy high in the air.

David grasped the steel mesh, got a toe hold, and scrambled to the top. He received no electric charge, the metal can had temporarily broken the circuit. Then he jumped, remembering to relax like a cat as he fell to the pavement.

An instant later Larry landed beside him and jerked him to his feet.

Almost before David knew what was happening they crossed Karl Marx Avenue and sought the shelter of a stone arcade. Behind them, in the railroad yard, at least a dozen armed men were shouting to each other as they combed the grounds.

The arcade was lined with shops, and beyond it, at the far end, was another street.

"If I remember my geography of Canton," Larry said as they walked swiftly toward the city, "that's the boulevard they've renamed for Mao Tse-tung."

They emerged onto the boulevard and suddenly found themselves in a mammoth crowd of laughing, excited people that lined both sides of the thoroughfare.

"Stay close beside me," Larry said, taking care to use the Cantonese dialect.

David nodded silently rather than answer in Mandarin or Hopeh. He had no idea what had caused the tremendous turnout of people, but felt momentarily safe in the huge throng. Then, as his father gently touched his arm, his feeling of security vanished. Directly ahead, about a block away, was a squad of soldiers carefully scrutinizing the people who streamed past them.

Larry turned to face the boulevard, and David did the same just as a band marched past. Behind it were rows of citizens, some carrying banners announcing a new "victory for communism." Canton, it seemed, was just like Peking, in that such parades were commonplace.

Here and there spectators were leaving the sidewalk and joining the march. Larry immediately took advantage of the situation and, telling David what to do with a tap and an inclination of the head, stepped off the curb.

They went to the middle of the line so they would be flanked by a screen of other marchers on both sides and fell in step. David felt like shouting for joy as they swept past the check point where the troops were studying the spectators. If a general alarm had been given for the fugitives, as seemed likely, no

241

one had yet thought of searching for them in the ranks of the paraders.

Father and son continued down Mao Tse-tung Boulevard, the rhythmic beat of drums and cymbals in their ears. The crowds of spectators, thicker and heavier as the paraders neared the heart of the business district, cheered lustily and applauded.

Larry made a careful inspection as he marched, and felt certain that a manhunt was in progress. Here and there brown-uniformed members of the Security Service, working in pairs, mingled with the throngs, and their determined manner indicated that they were searching for someone.

Shortly after they had passed beyond the city's business district Larry touched David on the shoulder and they left the line of march.

The crowds in this neighborhood were somewhat thinner and less boisterous. David saw the flags of various foreign nations fluttering from the masts of poles on a quiet side street and realized that these buildings must be the consulates of nations that maintained diplomatic relations with China.

Larry paused to buy two packets of water ice from a street vendor, then strolled toward the side street. Father and son looked like a leisurely pair enjoying a day's outing. They halted in shadows diagonally across the street from a building flying a white and red flag and stood there for the better part of half an hour, motionless and silent.

Then, as someone emerged from the building and walked to a car parked in front, Larry moved out of the shadows. "Now," he muttered, and went straight to the car.

The front door of the car closed just as Larry leaped into the back seat. "Don't make a sound, Laura," he told the woman who was settling herself behind the wheel.

Laura gasped as she felt the cold metal of an automatic press against the back of her neck.

David entered the car, and Larry climbed over the seat, taking his place beside the driver. "Take the Kowloon Road — to Hong Kong," he said.

14

LAURA GLANCED in the rear-view mirror and choked back a sob. "We're being followed."

"Of course," Larry said. "Ho F'ang's men want to escort you to the border."

"Why did you do this to me, Richie?"

"Turn left here, and then right."

"They undoubtedly have a two-way radio connecting them with their headquarters!" Her voice trembled. "There will soon be an alarm out for us, if there isn't already?"

"Now right again at this next corner. I want to avoid traffic wherever possible."

The car moved at a steady pace through the streets of Canton, closely followed by a larger vehicle, in which both the driver and his passenger, young men with athletic builds, wore civilian clothes.

"We'll have to get rid of them quickly now," Larry said, "before they try to force us to the curb. Head straight for that tunnel under the next intersection."

"But that would take us north, and Hong Kong is south!"

"Do as I tell you," Larry directed.

The car shot into the tunnel.

"No, Laura! Don't snap on your lights!"

The woman clung to the wheel, trying to peer through the gloom of the tunnel beneath the city's streets.

Ahead rumbled a truck, moving at a slow pace, and still only a few paces behind them was the other car.

"Pass the truck," Larry said. "Use his headlights for your own light. That's it. Go faster now. This tunnel is just a two-lane road, and you've got to pass him before that traffic coming the other way holds us up."

Laura barely managed to squeeze past the truck before several vehicles moving in the opposite direction blocked the other lane.

The Security Service men, furious because the truck now stood between them and the car they were following, began to honk their horn. They were so insistent that the driver of the truck became confused and slowed down.

Laura took her foot from the accelerator.

Larry raised his voice for the first time. "No! Step on it! Hard!"

The car rocketed and bounced forward across the badly paved road surface of the tunnel.

The horn was still sounding behind them, and David twisted in his seat. "The truck stopped," he said, "and the Security Service men still can't pass him."

"This is what I was gambling on," Larry said. "Laura, the end of the tunnel is directly ahead. Take a very sharp right turn as we come out."

She was preoccupied with her driving, but muttered, "You certainly must know Canton."

Larry had spent two days studying maps and aerial photographs of the area, and was grateful for the thoroughness of his training.

The blaring of the Security Service car's horn faded away as they emerged into the open.

Laura continued to follow directions, her face pale as she hunched over the wheel.

"Now," Larry said, "we're going to head toward the Hong Kong road. We're doubling back, but we're going to use short cuts instead of the main streets, and we'll pick up the highway again about ten miles beyond the suburbs." He concentrated on his directions.

There was little traffic on the streets they used, and they kept up a speed of about forty miles per hour.

David continued to stare out of the rear window. "There's nobody behind us. I think we've lost them."

"Good," his father said.

"What's so good about it?" Laura demanded. "There's sure to be an alarm out by now. They'll stop us at the Hong Kong border if they don't catch us before we reach it."

"I'm hoping," Larry replied gently, "that they believe we're heading north toward Shanghai again."

After another quarter of an hour they reached the highway, on which there was little traffic, and increased their speed to seventy miles per hour.

Larry finally broke a heavy, forty-minute silence. "Laura," he said, "I have no intention of compromising you with the Security Service any more than necessary. We seem to be in the clear — for the moment. David and I will leave you before we reach the border, and you can go on alone. If we aren't with you, they can't hold you. There will be no evidence against you."

"They'll still question me."

"Probably. But you can tell them that a couple of strangers demanded a lift, and that you dropped us off right in Canton. They won't be able to prove otherwise. And, as they don't want open trouble with your embassy, they'll let you go on."

They were approaching the border area now, and in the fields on both sides of the road were the temporary camps of emigrants who hoped to leave China and begin new lives for themselves in Hong Kong. Most dictatorships sealed their borders and refused to let their citizens leave, but Red China's policy was different. This vast, overcrowded land, with a population fast approaching the seven-hundred-million mark, found it more convenient to get rid of the discontented poor. The Communist party chiefs, the police, and other authorities found it easier to control the millions who remained when those courageous enough to leave with only the clothes on their backs were gone.

These emigrants, many of them whole families, had set up crude housekeeping arrangements in tattered cotton tents that stretched for miles along the canals and other waterways that separated the Chinese mainland from the British crown colony. Hong Kong had been inundated with refugees, and although the Chinese were glad to see the malcontents go, the British, who were trying desperately to cope with problems of unemployment, disease, and famine, allowed only relatively few refugees to enter Hong Kong at any given time.

Elaborate controls were established on both

side of the border. Whole companies of troops stood sentry duty at the Chinese check points, and British immigration officials and customs men, aided by the police, were stationed at the far sides of the connecting bridges to make sure that the flow of newcomers was orderly.

Following Larry's instructions, Laura slowed the car to a more sedate pace, drove past a refugee camp, and after going another half mile, pulled over to the side of the road. "The car is yours now, Laura. Thanks for the ride," Larry said. He motioned David out of the rear seat.

"What will you do now?" Laura asked.

"I think it better that you don't know too much. In a situation like this, it's wise to be ignorant of Bliss."

She smiled at his joke and held out her hand. "You have a genius for survival, Richie. I'll try not to worry about you."

"Please don't. Look after yourself. And good luck."

Laura waved to David, and the car started off down the road toward the border.

Larry stood for a moment. "That," he said, "is the end of Richard L. Bliss. Let's be moving on, son."

They started out across a bare, dry field, so parched that there were deep cracks in the topsoil, where nothing was growing except for limp weeds. David felt a sense of pressure and began to walk rapidly, but his father's hand touched his shoulder, restraining him.

"Not too fast," Larry told him. "No one hurries here. Some of these refugees wait as long as six months to cross the border."

The boy looked up at his father, eyes widening.

"But with luck, we'll be in Hong Kong tonight."

The sun set with almost dramatic abruptness, as it does in all lands located between the Tropic of Cancer and the equator. Daylight gave way to a soft blue-black haze, and then night came swiftly.

"They'll be watching for us at the customs gates," Larry said, "and I wouldn't be surprised if extra patrols are sent out all along the border. The Security Service doesn't know for certain that we'll try to get into Hong Kong, but it's the most logical haven for people in our position, so Ho F''ang is sure to have a strong force posted in the area."

"How will we avoid the patrols, Dad?"

"By doing what thousands of refugees do every year." Larry slapped at a mosquito that settled on his face and smiled. "We're near water at last. This is one time I welcome mosquitoes."

After walking another quarter of a mile Larry raised a cautioning hand. A rising half-moon revealed a cluster of buildings off to the right, and he and David made a wide detour to their left.

David studied the buildings and realized that they comprised a communal farm center. The ground was growing softer, spongier, and it occurred to him that they were approaching a rice field similar to one in which he had worked during a summer at a corrective labor camp.

Larry halted to remove his shoes and socks, and the boy did the same. Tying their shoes together by the laces, they slung them around their necks and walked silently on bare feet through a rice field partly submerged in water that oozed into it from a nearby bog. The moon disappeared behind a thick bank of clouds, and they picked their way more carefully.

The odors of rotting vegetation became stronger, and suddenly they found themselves in the swamp, calf deep in mud and water. Larry seemed to glide forward effortlessly without making a sound, and David, watching him, soon learned the trick. By taking short steps and not quite lifting his feet out of the slime he was able to make his way quietly too.

The march through the swamp seemed endless, but at last they came to dry ground beyond it. The moon was still hidden, but David could see now that a barren field stretched ahead, a desolate piece of land without trees or shrubbery. As he gazed at it, wishing they would stop so he could wipe the mud from his legs and feet, a dog barked in the distance.

Larry instantly threw himself to the ground, pulling David down with him.

The boy knew better than to ask any questions. Obviously it was necessary to maintain complete silence.

Again the dog barked, somewhat closer. Larry and David pressed close to the ground, and when the man reached for his pistol his son did the same.

The tension became almost unbearable. They saw something move on the far side of the field, and when the blur became distinguishable they made out the figures of two uniformed men, both armed with rifles. One held the leash of a large, shaggy-haired dog.

The breeze was slight, but it was blowing in the direction of the two fugitives, so the animal was unable to pick up their scent.

Neither moved until the guards and their dog vanished in the gloom. Then Larry hauled himself to his feet, and David quickly followed his example. "Now, son. Let's go!"

They sprinted across the field, Larry adjusting his pace to his son's shorter stride. They ran more than four hundred yards and were gasping for breath when huge coils of barbed wire loomed directly ahead. Here, at last, was the actual border; beyond it lay the British crown colony of Hong Kong — and safety.

David assumed that they would search for a break in the crude fence, but Larry found a piece of wood and used it to twist a wire until it separated.

"This will take us too long, son. I'd hoped we could make ourselves a path, but we'd need the rest of the night. We'll have to risk getting a few cuts."

He inched forward, the boy close behind him, and they wriggled carefully through the fence. Their clothes were ripped again and again, and David winced but made no sound when he felt his skin being pierced. Then all at once they were able to stand free of the barbs. They started forward again across a field as bare and uninviting as that on the far side of the fence.

"You, there! Halt!"

David stiffened as he heard a man shout in Cantonese.

Larry sighed quietly and smiled, silently repeating to himself the address and names in San Francisco that would enable General Hopkins to destroy a Chinese espionage center.

"Over here, sir! I've bagged two of them who have just come through!"

David relaxed, laughing aloud as he realized that the man was speaking English.

A smartly uniformed British officer in khaki shorts and shirt approached at a trot, followed by two soldiers.

Larry went forward to meet them, an arm around David's shoulders.